SOCCER SHOCK

SOCCER SHOCK

by **Donna Jo Napoli**

illustrated by Meredith Johnson

14,470

DUTTON CHILDREN'S BOOKS
NEW YORK

Library of Congress Cataloging-in-Publication Data

Napoli, Donna Jo, date.
    Soccer shock / by Donna Jo Napoli; illustrated by Meredith
Johnson.—1st ed.
        p. cm.
    Summary: When ten-year-old Adam discovers that his freckles can
see and talk, he plans to enlist their aid to get onto the school
soccer team.
    ISBN 0-525-44827-6
    [1. Soccer—Fiction.] I. Johnson, Meredith, ill. II. Title.
PZ7.N15So 1991
[Fic]—dc20   91-20706
                                                                   CIP
                                                                    AC

Published in the United States by Dutton Children's Books,
a division of Penguin Books USA Inc.
375 Hudson Street, New York, New York 10014

Designer: Joseph Rutt

Printed in U.S.A.   First Edition
10 9 8 7 6 5 4 3 2 1

For Barry, Elena, Michael,
Nicholas, Eva, and Robert, with love

CONTENTS

CHAPTER 1

The Shock

. . . .

Adam stood on the soccer field and twisted his hands together while Coach Morrison assigned them positions. He'd started out as left fullback at every practice since the school year began last week. Not a great position. But left fullback was better than not playing. There were only two positions left to assign, and there were still eight boys waiting for their assignments.

Coach Morrison stopped talking and folded his arms across his chest. "I don't like the looks of those clouds, guys." He twisted his mouth in indecision. "Hmmmm." He rocked back on his heels and watched the sky.

Adam looked up, too. The clouds weren't the black, lumpy storm clouds that drenched everyone in a flash. They were light grey and sort of smeared at the edges. And they were moving this way fast. Above them the sky was a watery pink, like someone had painted it.

Grayson, the tallest kid in fifth grade and the best player around, dribbled his soccer ball in a circle. "Can't we play at least a short scrimmage?"

Coach Morrison looked across the boys' faces and finally nodded. "Okay, let's try it. Michael, you're sweeper; Adam, left fullback. That's it for both sides. The rest of you boys start on the sidelines, and I'll rotate you in." Coach Morrison ran to the middle of the field and set down the soccer ball. "Let's play ball!" he shouted. He blew the whistle and Grayson kicked off.

The ball zipped onto Adam's side of the field, and Michael dashed up from the rear and took off with it. Milt followed and came up on the left for a pass. Adam watched the action, which was by now far away. He scratched his knees and happened to glance down. A hard-shell beetle crawled along the top edge of his right shoe. Adam looked across the field. The action was still thick and still far away. He stamped his feet and looked again. The beetle was now clinging to the knot on Adam's shoelaces. It was shiny black and about the size of his thumbnail. Adam thought he saw pincers coming out of its head. He danced in place. The beetle crawled onto his sock. Adam knew he should reach down and flick it off. Just one of those simple, fast flicks with the back of his hand. It would be easy. Except for those pincers. Adam held up his foot and shook hard. The beetle stuck fast. Adam held his foot higher and flung it wildly about.

At that very moment the ball came zooming his way, like a demon with his wings on fire. It bashed into Adam's left knee, bounced off, and Grayson had a perfect shot at a goal.

Adam watched the ball sail through the goalposts. He heard groans from the boys on his side. Some-one from behind him (Was it Clifford?) hissed, "What were you doing, Freckle Brain?" Adam hoped no one else had heard. He looked down at his speckled arms. When he was a little kid, people used to call him Freckles. But they stopped a couple of years ago. Adam didn't like his old nickname. He didn't want it back.

He scratched both knees. Then his arms. Then his back. He was itchy all over. Every time some-thing rotten happened to him, he got itchy.

"Okay, Gordon," shouted Coach Morrison, "ro-tate in for Adam."

The boys on the sidelines had organized their own mini-scrimmage behind the bleachers. Now they stopped and looked at Coach Morrison expectantly.

"Jim, go in there for Pete; Zach, take Jeff's place. Yeah, that's enough for now. Don't worry, guys," said the coach to the remaining three boys. "You'll all be worked in the next chance I get." He blew the whistle.

Adam walked off the field with Pete and Jeff. But while Pete and Jeff joined the rest of the boys on the sidelines, Adam sat down alone on the lowest level of the bleachers.

Kim came out from under the bleachers and stood in front of him. "Hi."

Adam looked past her at the game. He wondered what she was doing here. They'd never been in the same class before this year, so he hardly knew her. But she always seemed to be popping up lately. "Hi," he said.

Kim waited. She ran her thumbs around the inside of her belt. "October isn't very far away."

Adam thought about that. There didn't seem to be anything to say. He watched Gordon block a hard kick. Very nice move. Milt should have picked up on it, though. He should have been ready to take it and travel back up the field.

"The first Thursday of October, roller skating begins at the Super Rink." Kim moved over to block Adam's view. "It's going to be fun."

Adam slid along the bench till he could see the game again. That forward on the other side—Rick, yeah, that was his name—he was moving out from the crowd and looking around. He was obviously planning something. And no one on Adam's side seemed to notice. They had beter watch him. Adam wished he could shout out to his side's defense. But Coach Morrison didn't allow anything like that.

"I'm going." Kim moved over and blocked Adam's view again. "Are you?"

"Huh?"

"Roller skating," said Kim. "Now that we're in fifth grade, we're allowed to go to the Thursday night skating sessions. You know, in October. Are you going?"

"I don't think so." Adam leaned to the left and looked past Kim. He saw Grayson run directly toward Jeff as though he was going to zip by him on the left. At the last minute he dodged to the right, and Jeff couldn't block him. What a fantastic fake-out! He'd seen Grayson do that kind of a fake-out before, but every time he was impressed.

Kim tugged at her belt buckle. "You have a beetle

on your sock." She plucked it off and dropped it into her pants pocket. "For science lesson," she said, patting the pocket.

Adam looked at the moving bulge in Kim's pocket. That dumb bug had actually held on even when the ball hit him.

"Do you like bugs?" asked Kim.

Adam shrugged and shifted his eyes back to the soccer field.

"I don't really," she said, "but I want the extra credit. Anyway, bugs aren't that bad. It's spiders that are awful." She squeezed her hands together. "I hate spiders!" She waited. Finally she walked over to the huge oak tree and grabbed the round wooden swing that hung by a thick rope through a hole in its middle.

Last year someone had tossed the swing over a high branch, so it hung a good four feet off the ground when it used to hang only three feet off the ground. All the big kids liked it better that way, so the swing remained permanently four feet off the ground.

Kim was too short to jump onto the swing from the ground, even with a running start. So were most kids. To get onto the swing, Kim had to march up to the very top of the bleachers, pulling the swing behind her. She leaned out over the edge of the bleachers, with her hands as high up on the rope as she could reach, and pushed off, jumping onto the swing. Adam watched her sail past the tree, high off the ground.

Coach Morrison blew the whistle. "Rotation time, guys."

The boys who hadn't yet played filled in for the defense on both sides. Adam knew he wouldn't get rotated back in for at least another fifteen minutes. He got up and walked the fifty feet to the playground ladder, which stood outside his classroom window. Everyone went across it at recess, hanging by their hands. Adam had gone across it at least a hundred times. The wind was picking up now and it blew against his back. He swung himself to the middle of the ladder and did pull-ups. Adam was terrific at pull-ups. And at climbing, too. Adam's mother said he had great upper-body strength. Adam wished his lower body was as strong. What he wanted most of all was to be good at soccer.

Oh, it was fine to climb and do pull-ups. But those things weren't the same. Soccer took strategy. You had to think out each play and then be smart enough to change your strategy if the other side did something you didn't expect. It was a challenge, a beautiful challenge. Whenever Adam sat on the sidelines, he planned out the next move. Even on the field his mind knew what to do next. The problem was his body; it never did the right thing. Adam hadn't made the fourth-grade team last year, and he probably wouldn't make the fifth-grade team this year.

The air felt strangely heavy. The noises from the soccer field came to Adam as though through a megaphone, reverberating from far away. He dropped to the ground and turned around just as the sky filled with light.

Coach Morrison blew the whistle again and called the boys to the center of the field. "Sheet lightning. Get home fast before the rain hits." He looked around. "Anyone need a ride?" No one answered. He smiled. "Good scrimmage. See you tomorrow after school. Practice your dribbling at home, right?"

"Right," said the boys, hopefully. No one groaned. Everyone wanted to make that team. Every last one of them wanted to show Coach Morrison how dedicated he was.

Adam gathered up the soccer balls as the other boys walked home. He put them in Coach Morrison's canvas sack. "Can I do anything else to help out?"

"No, that's fine, Adam. Thanks. You better hurry along now." Coach Morrison picked up the sack and swung it over his shoulder.

"Coach?"

"What is it, Adam?"

"Do I have a chance at making the team?"

"You want an honest answer?"

Adam knew that question was bad news. Honest answers were always bad news. But now that he had asked for it, he couldn't very well say no. He nodded his head.

"Everyone has a chance," Coach Morrison said. That meant Adam had no chance at all. Then he went on, "But you would have a better chance if you paid more attention. You missed that last ball because you were goofing off."

"That was a mistake," Adam said. He thought about the beetle, now snug in Kim's pocket. He wondered if it was pinching her thigh right now. "I only looked away for a minute."

"You need to watch where the other team is, keep your eyes on the ball, anticipate what's going to happen, be ready for the next move." Coach Morrison walked as he talked. "You've got to work harder, Adam. That's all there is to it." The wind was so strong now, the coach was practically yelling in Adam's direction. "We started last week with three dozen boys trying out. Now we're down to twenty-eight. But only eighteen can be on the team. That's regulations." They reached the coach's car. "Only eighteen." Coach Morrison got in his car and drove off.

As Adam turned away, the wind came full in his face and made him feel invigorated and excited, in spite of the fact that Coach Morrison had practically told him he'd never make the team. He lifted his chin and enjoyed the smell of storm in the air. His father always said Michigan knew how to do a storm right. Adam reached the corner of Oxford Street before he heard the first thunder. It cracked from behind, from somewhere way off near the university. Then he saw a flash toward his house. He counted, knowing that for every full five seconds before the thunder sounded, the lightning was a mile away. The thunder boomed before Adam counted to three. He ran now. The rain came pelting down. He decided to cut across the woods in the arboretum to save time. He ran as fast as he could.

That's when it happened. The lightning flash came down in front of him with blinding intensity. The thunder sounded at the same time. Adam was hurled to the ground. He lay on his back with his eyes closed. His skin tightened and prickled up his

10

arms and legs, across his chest and back, up his temples. He could feel his arm hairs stand on end. His ears rang.

He stayed that way for what seemed like a very long time. I'm not dead, thought Adam as the rain made puddles in his eye sockets. It didn't hit me. I'm not dead. The ringing in his ears got slightly softer. I'm not dead.

"He's not dead," said a voice, coming up through the ringing noise, as if in echo.

"I know that," said a second voice with irritation. "If he was dead, we'd be dead."

Adam wanted to shout, "Who's there?" But his face felt like lead. He couldn't move his mouth. Tiny stars of light danced inside his eyelids. They made him feel dizzy. The ringing was now background noise, and the voices stood out sharply against it.

"He's quite fortunate, you know," said the first voice. "Ten feet closer and the shock wave would have been strong enough to stop his heart."

"Oh, yeah, here comes the long story. As if you know anything, Gilbert."

The voice called Gilbert made a little snort. "I happen to have paid attention to that television program on electricity two nights ago. We were right there in the living room, remember?"

"Yeah, yeah. And now comes the part about eons, huh?"

"*Ions,*" said Gilbert, "not *eons.* Eons are long periods of time. You'd know that, Frankie, if you'd pay attention even half the time."

By now the ringing in Adam's ears had all but faded away, and as it faded, the voices got weaker.

"You know what you are, Gilbert? A stuck-up brain who thinks he knows something. But you don't know nothing. You're as gooney as the kid."

"All right, that's it," said Gilbert in what sounded to Adam like the faintest whisper. "I've . . ."

Adam could no longer make out the words. He strained to hear the voices. Nothing. He pulled all his energy together and managed to sit up. He forced his eyes open and looked around, searching through the rain to see who was talking. There was no one there. He got up slowly and looked in every direction. Gilbert and Frankie, whoever they were, were nowhere in sight. He called out, "Where are you?" No one answered.

Adam's body shook with shivers.

CHAPTER 2

Discovery

. . . .

Adam was waterlogged by the time he got home. He stood in the front hall and dripped a puddle onto the wood floor.

Catherine, his big sister, looked over at him from the dining room, where she was setting the table. "Adam, what's the matter with you? You're white as a ghost."

Suddenly fatigue overwhelmed him. Adam sank down onto his knees. Then he crumpled forward into a heap.

"Mamma!" screamed Catherine in a frantic voice. "Mamma!"

Mamma came rushing in from the kitchen. Adam lifted his chin and gave her a weak smile. She took one look at him and left, returning a few seconds later with a towel. "Get those wet clothes off." She was already rubbing his hair with the towel. "What happened to you?"

"I got caught in the rain."

"I can see that. Coach Morrison never should have had you practicing in the rain."

"He sent us home before the rain hit," said Adam in a hoarse voice. "But I wasn't fast enough. And then there was the lightning."

Mamma stopped rubbing. "Lightning?"

"It struck right in front of me."

Mamma sat back on her heels and pulled Adam onto her lap. "Did you get hurt?"

"I don't think so. I mean, I fell down on my back and I couldn't get up for a while."

Mamma slid Adam off her lap. "Stay right here." She ran into the kitchen.

Catherine stared at Adam as they both listened to Mamma call the doctor. Then they heard Mamma's heels click up the back stairs. She came racing down a moment later.

"Okay," said Mamma, pulling on her raincoat and holding out one to Adam. "Wet and all, let's go. We'll be back just as soon as we can."

Twenty minutes later, Adam sat with his shirt off as Dr. Rizzoli finished the examination.

"Guess you can change into those dry clothes your mom brought." Dr. Rizzoli smiled at Adam.

Then he turned to Adam's mother. "This young man is lucky to be alive."

Mamma's eyes filled with tears.

"Oh, I didn't mean to scare you. The lightning bolt discharged a massive amount of electricity in the air around Adam, but it didn't do him any permanent damage. If it had been *really* close, he'd have lost his memory, at least."

Tears ran down Mamma's cheeks.

Dr. Rizzoli looked alarmed. "There, there. The tingling in his skin, the way his hair stood up, the ringing in his ears, all that is perfectly normal given the situation. They are all products of the fact that the air was electrically charged. Adam is going to be fine, just fine."

"Is it normal to hear voices when you're almost struck by lightning?" asked Adam, pulling his dry shirt over his head.

"Voices!" said Mamma.

"Voices?" said Dr. Rizzoli.

"Voices," said Adam.

Dr. Rizzoli snuck a glance at Mamma. She was staring at him. He straightened up and put a cheerful look on his face as he spoke loudly and firmly to Adam. "Your eardrums received a charge and they might act funny for a while. They've been sensitized. Sometimes people who are almost hit by lightning report hearing noises we can't normally hear—like the sound of their own heartbeat or the sound of the blood rushing through their veins."

"I heard voices," said Adam, "not my heart and not my blood."

Mamma sniffled.

Dr. Rizzoli cleared his throat. "I'm sure it's nothing. Don't worry. You won't be hearing any more strange voices." He patted Adam on the shoulder. "And good luck making that soccer team."

Mamma thanked Dr. Rizzoli. Then they drove back through the steady rain.

"I was going to make baked macaroni and cheese tonight. I already grated the cheese," said Mamma. "But it can wait till tomorrow. Tonight let's have whatever you want, Adam." She smiled over at Adam. "What do you want?"

Adam brightened. "Pizza."

And so they came home with a pepperoni pizza and a large bottle of Coke. Daddy and Catherine and Nora, Adam's little sister, were waiting when they got home.

Daddy's arms circled Adam tightly. "So how's my wet athlete?"

"I'm dry now."

"Dr. Rizzoli said he's going to be fine," said

Mamma. "It struck just far enough away from him that he escaped real harm."

"Let's eat the pizza while it's hot," said Catherine.

Adam sat at the table in his usual seat beside Nora.

"Guess how many teddy bears I have in my bed," said Nora to Daddy.

"Ummm," said Daddy, pouring Coke for everyone. "How many?"

"One," said Nora.

Everyone laughed.

Nora looked confused.

"You missed the point," said Catherine. "You don't ask people to guess if what they're guessing at isn't special."

"John is a special bear," said Nora.

"You missed the point again," said Catherine. "It isn't . . ."

Catherine's words suddenly seemed far away. They blended together in a fine buzz. Adam found himself drifting away from the conversation. He closed his eyes and remembered how it felt to lie there in the woods. Gilbert and Frankie. Dr. Rizzoli had said not to worry: There wouldn't be any more strange voices. But Adam wasn't worried; he was curious. He wanted to know who those voices belonged to.

Adam went over the conversation in his head for the tenth time, at least. One of them, Frankie, had said that if Adam had died, they'd have died, too. That was a remarkable thing to say. Why would Adam's death kill anyone else? There was no reason. No one else depended on Adam that much. If Adam died, Adam died. That's all.

"Adam? Are you okay? Adam!"

Adam blinked several times and focused on his mother.

"See?" Mamma said, turning to Daddy. "There really might be something wrong with his ears." She looked at Adam hard. "Was it those voices again?"

"Not exactly," said Adam.

Mamma looked at Daddy. "I think he needs a thorough hearing check."

"Didn't you just tell me that Dr. Rizzoli said his eardrums might act funny for a while? Let's relax about it. If he's still hearing things a week from now, we'll call Dr. Rizzoli and see what the next step is, okay?"

"Okay," said Mamma doubtfully.

They cleared the table and everyone went about their usual after-dinner business. For Adam that meant his homework, which he did at the dining room table.

Adam intended to concentrate. But he couldn't

help thinking about the voices again. His mind was filled with questions. Who were Gilbert and Frankie? And why had Adam heard them right at that moment? Right when lightning had just struck? Dr. Rizzoli thought it was his eardrums—they'd been sensitized—and now they allowed him to hear things he couldn't normally hear. But that didn't explain who the voices were. And anyway, if it was just that Adam's eardrums had changed and nothing else, then surely he'd still be hearing the voices now. But he wasn't. The voices had ended when the ringing in his ears ended.

There had to be a reason for that. Maybe there was a connection between the ringing and the voices. Dr. Rizzoli said the electrical charge in the air caused the ringing. So probably the ringing in his ears ended when the electricity in the air dissipated. That meant Adam could hear the voices only when the air was electrically charged. So electricity had something to do with it all.

Electricity carries voices in telephone wires by making a circuit between the voices on either end. A circuit. Maybe the electricity had somehow made some kind of a circuit between the voices and Adam's eardrums.

Okay, maybe. Adam got excited. That made sense. That meant that there were voices out there somewhere that Adam could hear with his new, changed eardrums. If only Adam could make that circuit again, he could hear them. He needed to make that circuit. Gilbert and Frankie were important. They seemed to depend on Adam for their life. He had to know who they were. And besides, Frankie had accused Gilbert of being a brain. Adam knew that accusation only too well. Adam was the math star of his grade. If Gilbert was a brain, Adam wanted to know him.

So Adam had to figure out a way to form a circuit between his ears and the voices.

Gilbert wasn't the only one who had listened to the TV program on electricity Sunday night. Adam had listened, too. He knew how to make a circuit. All he needed to do was find a good conductor and attach it to the two terminals. There were all sorts of good conductors around. Any metal was a conductor. The problem was the terminals. Okay, at one end he had his eardrums. But the problem was the other end. He didn't know where those voices were coming from.

If the voices were with Adam on Sunday night and if the voices would have died if Adam had died, that meant the voices were close to him. Maybe they formed some sort of aura around him, like an angel's halo.

Adam drew a picture of himself on his math homework with a ring of light around his head. He smiled.

But it seemed impossible to connect a conductor from his eardrums to a halo he couldn't see. The conductor would have to be really big—big enough to go all around his head and touch that halo, wherever it might be.

"Finish up, Adam," said his mother, on her way upstairs. "It's getting late."

Adam erased the picture of himself with a halo and finished his math homework. Then he walked up the stairs, reciting to himself all the metals he could think of: copper, silver, gold, platinum, nickel, steel, aluminum, iron. He couldn't very well set his head in a bed of iron or gold. No, metals wouldn't do it.

Gases could be conductors if they were heated to a high enough temperature. But Adam wasn't about to put his head into a container of hot gases.

So metals and gases were out. He needed something that wasn't hard like metal and didn't need to be hot like gas.

Of course: Water!

Within thirty seconds Adam was sitting in the tub. He could hear Catherine and Nora playing in the bedroom they all shared down the hall. His hearing seemed to be working all right. Okay, you sensitized ears, thought Adam, do your stuff.

Adam slid down till the warm water hit him mid-chest. He listened hard. He heard the slow drip of water from the tub faucet. *Plink. Plink.* He slid down farther, till his ears were in the water. Only his mouth and nose and eyes were dry now. He could no longer hear his sisters. Even the *plink* had turned to a dull *plud.* It was quiet. He shut his eyes and concentrated. He could hear his heart pumping. He could hear his lungs expanding as they took in air. He listened hard.

"What are you complaining about?" said a wavery voice.

Adam sat up with a start. His heart beat fast. He could hear his sisters' voices from the bedroom. He could hear the clicking of his father's typewriter. But those sounds were out there. The bathroom was empty. He hardly dared to think it, but somewhere from the back of his mind came the tiny whisper: Maybe it's working.

Adam slid back down till his head was once more in the water.

"I received a most unfortunate blow at soccer today. It was quite a spectacle," said another wavery voice.

"Who cares, after what we've been through with

lightning?" said the first voice. "Anyway, Gil, it was nothing compared to what happened to me when the clod climbed the ash tree yesterday."

Adam sat up. He was breathing hard. "Who's there?" he called. He got out of the tub and dripped his way to the door. He peeked out into the hall. No one.

Adam went back in the tub again. He waved his arms through the air above his head, half expecting to hit a hot halo. There was nothing there. He jerked his shoulders. He scratched his knees. Then he slid down till his ears were underwater again.

"That scratching felt simply marvelous," said the voice Adam thought was Gilbert. The wavery quality of the voices had to be due to the tub water.

"No fair," said Frankie. "Every time something bad happens, he scratches you first, and harder, too."

Adam lifted his head out of the water. The voices stopped. Adam was sure now that the voices weren't coming from other rooms. They weren't even coming from the bathroom. The voices were in the tub with him. And not just in the water. They were in his body. He was positive. Gilbert and Frankie lived in Adam. Like parts of his body. They felt it when he scratched his knees. In fact, it seemed almost as if his knees were talking—as if that was possible.

What a stupid idea. He didn't even bother to look at his knees. There was nothing there except a few freckles. Nothing that could talk.

A few freckles. That's all. Freckles.

"Well, neither of us has gotten enough hard scratching lately," said Gilbert. "He's worn long pants all week. Must be an early autumn."

"Of course it's an early autumn," said Frankie. "He took us rolling in leaves just yesterday. You don't get piles of leaves all over the ground unless it's autumn, Gilbert. You know, you're not as smart as everyone thinks, in spite of your fancy talk."

Adam bent his legs till his knees were out of the water. The voices stopped. He lowered his knees.

"I'm getting rather chilly with all this in and out of the water," said Gilbert.

"Maybe be's doing some stupid knee exercise," said Frankie.

Adam sat up. Now he did look at his knees. He looked closely. The bruise on his left knee was starting to turn into a black-and-blue mark. Near the edge of the bruise was his favorite freckle. The scrape on his right knee was no longer raw. It had spots of scab. Between two spots of scab was another freckle. Well, it was a ridiculous idea, but he had to test it. The freckles were the one thing both knees had in common. He had to test whether the voices came from them. Adam pressed his finger on the freckle on his right knee. Then he slid down till his ears were underwater. He had to twist to the right to keep his finger in place.

"Oh, dear, what's going on over there?" said Gilbert.

There was no answer.

"Can't you hear me?" asked Gilbert.

Adam lifted his finger.

"He was pressing on me," said Frankie. "Maybe his scabs hurt."

Adam stood up. He looked in the mirror above the sink. He didn't look crazy. Or at least no crazier than usual. He wondered if almost being hit by lightning made you crazy. He blinked at himself in the mirror. He squinted. He cocked an eyebrow. Then he noticed the cluster of small freckles on his right shoulder.

Adam lay down in the water and contorted himself until his right shoulder was close to his knees.

"Why, hello, up there, you pretty little freckles!" called Gilbert. "Franklin and I take pleasure in greeting you again."

"I'm Frankie, not Franklin," said Frankie gruffly. "And you're just looking for trouble, talking to them. Don't you remember how they acted last time?"

"Freckles? *Humpf*," said a high-pitched voice. "We've told you before and we'll tell you again: We're beauty marks, not freckles. And we'd greatly appreciate it if you'd keep your attentions to yourselves."

"See?" said Frankie. "Snobs. Why, they're just a bunch of specks. Forget them."

Adam straightened out. His heart was beating so hard, he thought it might burst. This couldn't be happening. Then he remembered the big freckle on the bottom of his left foot. At the inner sole. He put his left foot on his right knee, making sure the freckles hit one another, and he lay back.

Adam thought he heard some muffled growlings. He lifted his foot a little.

"Hey! What's the big idea?" shouted Frankie.

"Look, I don't know. It's the boy. Blame him, not me," the foot freckle shouted back.

"Well, don't let it ever happen again," said Frankie, "or I'll mash you!"

The foot freckle laughed. "How're you going to do that, Knee Spot? I'm the one that stomps on things!"

Adam straightened his leg. He was stunned with the mixed emotions of disbelief and tremendous excitement.

His mother peeked into the bathroom. "Time for

bed, Adam." She plopped a fresh towel on the top of the stool. "Do you realize what time it is already? And after the day you've had, you need your rest. Hurry up."

Adam lay in bed. His pillow touched the windowsill, and the edges of the curtain rested on the pillowcase. He stuck his head under the curtain and looked at the streetlight on the corner. His little sister was already asleep. His big sister was now in the dining room finishing her homework. The bedroom was quiet.

Adam listened as hard as he could.

He stared at the bottom of the bunk above his. It was time to appraise the situation. Adam was not a crazy kid. He wasn't even imaginative. His teachers had always praised him at math but always told him to be more creative in art. They told him to let go, be more flamboyant, develop his imagination. But Adam didn't seem to have any imagination to develop. So right now he had to face facts: His freckles talked. They talked to each other. Those little brown spots all over his body actually talked to each other. And what was even more marvelous was that Adam could hear them. The lightning had changed his eardrums, and with the help of a conductor he could listen to Gilbert and Frankie. Now any time he took a bath he could hear them. Any time he went swimming, he could hear them. Maybe even any time he got drenched in a rainstorm he'd be able to hear them. The water, which had always been silent before, would now be filled with voices.

Adam lay as still as he could in the dark bedroom. The discovery overwhelmed him. He wondered how much his freckles knew. He wondered how much they could do. He shut his eyes and tried to relax totally. Maybe if all his muscles were relaxed, he'd be able to hear the voices even without the help of water. After all, his ears were special now. Adam concentrated on his freckles and listened hard.

Nothing.

Adam scratched one knee.

Nothing.

He scratched both knees.

More nothing.

There was no way around it: He simply couldn't hear them out here in the air. Adam looked at his fingers. They were still wrinkled from the bath water. If he sat in the tub all day, he would turn into a pickle. No, he had to find some other way to hear his freckles talk. Some other way.

CHAPTER 3

Math Lesson

· ·

Adam woke up with the feeling that he had something important and urgent to do. Slowly the events of yesterday came back into his memory. His life had changed yesterday. He now had two goals instead of one: to get on the soccer team and to find a way to listen to Gilbert and Frankie. The first goal would have to wait till practice after school. But he could start on the second goal right now.

He got out of bed and walked straight to his bureau. Adam opened the top drawer and stared at the contents, hoping an idea would come to him.

"What're you looking for?" said Nora. She sat on the edge of her bed and struggled to get her feet into ballet slippers that were obviously too small for her.

"None of your business."

31

"Oh." Nora gave up on the shoes and walked over to the windowsill where Fancy, their big, fat cat, lay stretched out in the morning sun. She put a ballet slipper on Fancy's front left paw. It fell off. "Can I borrow some of your tape?"

"Tape shoes on a cat?" Adam threw up his hands in disgust. "You're a dumbbell." He turned back to the drawer. Tape on a cat. And with all of Fancy's thick yellow fur. Tape. Tape! That was it! Adam shuffled through the drawer wildly.

"Well, can I?" asked Nora. "Can I?"

Under the pile of bottle caps Adam found a plastic frog, a sock with a hole in the heel, and, finally, his roll of transparent tape. Maybe tape would act as a conductor. Who knew what was in it? Yeah. Anyway, it was worth a try. It was the best idea he had right now. Adam grabbed some clothes and ran with the tape to the bathroom, never bothering to answer Nora's stupid question. He shut the door.

Adam slipped out of his pajamas and pressed tape onto his favorite freckle—the one he now knew was named Gilbert—and ran it up his left leg, up his torso, up his neck, and straight to his left ear. Then he pressed tape onto the freckle on his right knee—Frankie—and ran it all the way up to his right ear. He put on his clothes, being careful not to move his head. He didn't want to unstick the tape. When he was dressed, he looked in the mirror. The tape to his ears showed. He turned up the collar on his shirt. Still, the tape showed a little.

"What are you doing in there?" asked Catherine.

"Huh?" Adam jumped at her voice and turned his head abruptly. The tape unstuck from both ears. He muttered under his breath, "Nosy sisters."

"Did you say something?" Catherine came in and grabbed the toothpaste. "Is that tape on your neck and ears?"

"Tape?" Adam looked back in the mirror. He rolled the ends of the tape down and hid them under his collar. Then he pocketed the rest of the roll of tape.

Catherine brushed her teeth and watched him. Adam picked up his toothbrush.

Catherine spat out some foam. "What's up?"

"I'll tell you later." Adam finished brushing and left.

"Hi," said Kim, appearing beside Adam.

Adam stepped back. He hadn't seen her coming. How had she managed to just pop up like that?

"Here." She held out her fist, opened it just long enough for Adam to have a look at the twisted cricket, and closed it again fast. "I decided the beetle was yours, so you should get the extra credit. But I left it in my pocket and Mom washed it dead. So I caught you a cricket instead."

Adam looked around again. Gordon was across the street. Adam always walked with Gordon. They'd walked to school together since kindergarten. It was habit. On the way, they picked up all sorts of things from the ground for their various collections. Lost marbles. Used-up matchbooks. Now and then a broken lighter. Kim might say the things they picked up were junk. No, Adam didn't think Gordon would like the addition of Kim. "Look, keep the cricket. I've got to go."

"I knew you didn't like bugs." Kim stuffed the cricket into her pocket. "So what kind of animals do you like?"

"Huh?" said Adam, his eyes on Gordon. Gordon was watching for a break in the traffic now. Pretty soon he'd be beside them.

"Well," said Kim, "do you like snakes?"

"I hate snakes."

"Lizards?"

"Yeah," said Adam. "Sure. Lizards. I've got to go now."

"Me, too." Kim ran ahead.

Adam had expected it would be hard to get rid

of her. Instead, she scooted behind a clump of bushes and she was out of sight already.

"Hi," said Gordon.

"Hi."

"What's with Kim?" asked Gordon.

"She wanted to give me a half-dead cricket."

"Pretty weird," said Gordon.

"Yeah."

Fifteen minutes later Adam opened his school desk and found himself face-to-face with a lizard. It sat on top of his science book, flicking its tiny tongue in and out of its mouth. Adam knew his only hope was to move fast. But he had to be careful; he knew lizards' tails broke off easily if you weren't gentle. He swooped his hand down near the hind legs and got it by the tail. Adam picked it up gingerly and looked around.

The window nearest him was closed. It was a super early fall in Michigan. The radiators had already begun to blast out their heat in mid-September. The only open window in the whole classroom was the one near Ms. Werner's desk. Adam walked slowly up to the front of the room and set the lizard on the outside ledge of the open window.

Ms. Werner looked up at Adam from her desk. "Is that a lizard?"

"I think so," said Adam. The lizard sat quietly on the window ledge, as though it didn't quite know what to do. Adam had never seen a lizard act so slow. When he chased them on the wall around the supermarket parking lot in the summer, they were almost always too fast to catch.

Ms. Werner stood up, walked to the window, and looked at the lizard. "Where did it come from?"

"I found it in my desk."

"You found a lizard in your desk?"

"Uh-huh."

Ms. Werner stared at Adam. "You found a lizard in your desk on this cold, cold morning?" Her tone of voice told it all: She didn't believe him. She looked back at the lizard. "He isn't moving. Is something the matter with him?"

Adam shrugged his shoulders.

"Well . . ." She looked around. "I wish I had a jar to put him in so everyone could have a good look at him." She sighed. "I guess you better give him a little nudge so he'll run off. And make sure he goes *out,* not *in.* Then get back to your desk."

Adam raised his hand to give the lizard a little shove. Just then the lizard sprang into action and leapt onto the playground ladder outside the window. It clutched at the slippery metal rung and scrambled to keep hold. It fell off and disappeared into the small pile of wet leaves below. Adam looked at Ms. Werner. She was watching him. He went back to his desk. On the way he passed Kim's desk. She looked down and whispered under her breath, "You said you liked lizards."

"Huh?" said Adam, taking his seat.

"You threw away a perfectly good lizard." She scowled at him. "It took me ten minutes to catch."

Adam felt confused. He hadn't meant to throw away a lizard.

"Math time, students." Ms. Werner smiled and armed herself with yellow chalk.

Adam felt better. Fifth-grade math was fun. This year there was a new method of teaching math. Ms. Werner's class had been chosen to experiment with it because Ms. Werner was said to be excellent at teaching math. Adam liked being part of something new and special.

Ms. Werner busily filled the blackboard with pictures of fish. There was one giant fish, named Goldie. And there were two schools of little fish. Underneath each school of little fish, Ms. Werner had put the number of fish in that school. Goldie always ate the school with the most little fish, so long as she could gobble them up in a certain number of gulps with none left over at the end. The children's job was to figure out which school Goldie would eat. Goldie wanted to take gulps of six fish at a time today.

It was a babyish game, Adam knew. Ms. Werner used to teach fourth grade instead of fifth, and sometimes it showed. But it was fun anyway. Adam knew right away that Goldie would pick the smaller school—it had twelve fish in it.

Ms. Werner stood patiently, looking for the first hand to pop up. Adam decided not to answer. It was too easy. He liked real challenges. He looked over at Kim. She was busy sharpening a crayon.

Susanna waved her hand. Hers was almost always the first hand to go up. Her father taught at the university, and everyone said she had to be competitive to keep her father happy. "The small school!" she said proudly.

"That's right, Susanna," said Ms. Werner. "Very good. And now, who can tell us why? How about you, Grayson?"

Grayson sat at the desk behind Adam's and shifted in his seat. He stretched his long legs out into the aisle and then quickly tucked them back under his seat. "Uhhhh."

"Maybe you could begin by looking at the small school and telling us how many gulps Goldie will take," said Ms. Werner.

Grayson rubbed his nose and looked out the window toward the soccer field.

From the other side of the room someone whispered, "Dumbo."

Ms. Werner snapped her head around. The room was suddenly silent. "There will be no name-calling in this room. Not today. Not tomorrow. Not ever. We treat each other with respect." Her cheeks were mottled pink and white. Her eyes glittered. "Grayson," said Ms. Werner with forced cheerfulness, "let's start at the beginning. If Goldie . . ." Ms. Werner's voice droned on as she began her usual routine of gentle questions. Adam had already become accustomed to the way she tried to lead students through to the right answer. She was encouraging and patient. He liked her. But sometimes it was boring to listen to that particular routine.

Adam slid down in his seat till the back of his neck hit the top of the back of his desk chair. The tape made a crackling noise. He wondered what his freckles were doing now. He unrolled the tape under his collar and attached it to his ears. He closed his eyes and listened. Nothing. Probably tape couldn't conduct little freckle voices after all. Adam looked around. Ms. Werner was still droning on about Goldie's first meal of the day. Adam smoothed the tape over his ear. Maybe it wasn't on tight enough. That might be the problem. He pressed it along his neck and down his sides. Still no sound. He leaned out and looked at his knees under his desk. Suddenly he knew what the problem was. He had on long pants. The freckles were covered. They were probably asleep. Even if the tape was a terrific conductor, he wouldn't be able to hear the freckles if they were sleeping. Carefully he rolled his right pant leg up over his knee.

"Ah, what a beautiful day," said Frankie.

Adam rolled up his left pant leg above the knee.

"Good afternoon," called Gilbert.

"It's still morning," said Frankie. "He's in math class. Don't you remember how much fun we had in math class when the weather was still hot? We need an Indian summer so that he can wear shorts to school again soon."

"Which brings us right to the point," said Gilbert. "Why on earth did he roll up his pants?"

"Who cares?" said Frankie. "Now at least we can see what's going on. Oh, look!"

"My word! What a plump piece of gum that is, stuck on the bottom of Kim's desk."

Adam looked up. Ms. Werner was drawing arrows between the circles of fish on the blackboard. It was safe to explore what the freckles were talking about. He leaned down and looked under Kim's desk.

Kim hit Adam on the top of the head. "What are you doing?"

Adam rubbed the spot where she'd whacked him. "There's purple gum under your desk. Want some?" He scratched it off the desk and held it out to her. It was still slightly soft.

Kim grabbed the gum. "That's mine and you better not touch it again." She put it back in place and gave Adam a stony glare. "First you throw away a perfectly good lizard. Then you try to steal my gum. You know, you're nothing but a big bother."

"Adam and Kim," said Ms. Werner from the front of the class. "No chatting now. Please pay attention."

Adam sat up a little and watched Ms. Werner erase some of the fish out of one school and draw some new ones in the other school. He figured out that Goldie would eat the school on the left; then he slid down in his seat again and listened.

"It's crawling faster now," said Frankie.

"I think it smells the gum," said Gilbert.

"What's crawling faster?" asked Adam out loud.

Kim glared at Adam. "I told you not to bother me."

"Something's going to get your gum," said Adam.

"Not you!" Kim grabbed the lump of gum, which had a small spider clinging to it. She was about to put it inside her desk when she saw the spider. "Ahhh!" The spider seemed to fly off the gum. It landed on Kim's lap. "Ahhh!" screamed Kim, standing up. The spider fell to the floor and disappeared.

Ms. Werner rushed up. "What's the matter?"

"Adam put a spider on me!" Kim pointed at Adam.

"What? No, I didn't," said Adam.

"Then how did you know it was there?" said Kim.

Adam didn't answer.

"See!" said Kim. "I knew you did it! And after I told you I hate spiders!"

Ms. Werner looked sternly at Adam. "Where is the spider now?" She was standing in the aisle between Adam's and Kim's desks. Adam couldn't see the back of her, but Frankie and Gilbert could.

"It's going up the back of her stocking," said Frankie.

"It's going up the back of your stocking," said Adam.

Ms. Werner stood perfectly still. She got a funny look on her face. Then she ran from the classroom. The children heard a muffled scream from the hall. Ms. Werner returned a few moments later, red in the face and walking quickly. She went right to Adam's desk.

"Adam, how did you know the spider was on the back of my leg?" Ms. Werner's voice was low and steady.

Adam looked at her without a word.

"Did you put the spider on me?" Ms. Werner's voice trembled a little now.

"No. No, I didn't."

"Stand up, please."

Adam stood up. Ms. Werner looked down at his rolled-up pants. Adam looked down, too. A bit of tape showed on each knee.

"Is that tape on your knees?"

Adam nodded.

Ms. Werner looked closely at Adam's neck and ears, where more tape showed. "And tape on your ears?"

"I guess so."

Ms. Werner looked again at Adam's rolled-up pants. Her face was bewildered. She looked almost sad. "Please roll your pants down and sit down," Ms. Werner said weakly.

"Okay."

As Adam rolled down his pant legs, Ms. Werner looked around. The whole class was watching. Ms.

Werner closed her eyes for a moment and gave a little shudder. "No more spiders, Adam," she said almost in a whisper.

"But I didn't put it on you," Adam whispered back.

"Right now, all I want is a promise. No more spiders."

"Okay," said Adam.

"And no more lizards. No more animals of any kind."

"Okay," said Adam. He could hear a giggle here and there around the classroom. He looked at Kim, intending to let her know that she better pay attention to Ms. Werner's words, too. After all, she was the one who caught the lizard. She should feel sorry. But when he looked at Kim, he got a surprise. She was staring at him with wide, shining eyes. And there was something unusual in her stare. Awe. She was staring at him with awe, as though he were an alien from another planet. As he looked at her, she gave a sort of half smile, nervously, as though there was something dangerous in smiling at him.

Adam's face was hot. Maybe listening to his freckles at school was a bad idea. At recess time he would go into the bathroom and take off the tape.

CHAPTER 4

Recess

. . . .

"All right, Adam." Ms. Werner smiled and tapped her pencil against her left hand. "Your turn. What can you tell us about current events?"

Adam's heart fell. He had forgotten to watch the news on TV after dinner last night. Every Tuesday night the class was supposed to watch the news on TV. But Adam had almost been struck by lightning Tuesday afternoon, and who could watch the news after a thing like that? All through this lesson, he had been silently willing Ms. Werner not to call on him. And now he was stuck. Adam looked at Ms. Werner blankly.

Ms. Werner smiled encouragingly. "Can you tell us about something local, perhaps?" She tapped her pencil a little faster. "What about the Tigers? Can you tell us what just happened to them?"

45

Adam thought hard. Tigers. Hmmmm. "At the zoo, you mean?"

Some of the children laughed. Ms. Werner put her finger to her lips and hushed them. "No, I mean the baseball team, the Detroit Tigers."

Baseball. Adam didn't know anything about baseball. His family never watched sports on TV. The only team sport Adam cared anything about was soccer.

"Adam?" said Ms. Werner.

Adam looked up blankly.

Kim hissed out of the side of her mouth. "Pssst."

Adam turned to Kim.

"Did you have something to say, Kim?" asked Ms. Werner.

Kim shook her head.

"Do you know what happened to the Detroit Tigers, Kim?"

"They won," said Kim. She turned in her seat and shrugged apologetically at Adam. But that new look of awe was in her eyes again, like when the spider had gone up Ms. Werner's leg.

"And who did they win against?" Ms. Werner's eyes were on Kim now.

Kim screwed up her mouth. She sat on her hands and rocked in her seat in worry.

Suddenly a piece of paper appeared on Adam's desk with words scrawled on it. Adam blurted out, "The Milwaukee Brewers."

"That's right, Adam," said Ms. Werner happily. "So you did do your current events homework, after all. Very good. Okay, class, you may walk quietly to the back of the room and get your jackets from the hooks. It's recess time."

Adam quickly folded the piece of paper with *Milwaukee Brewers* written on it and stuck it in his pocket. He looked around to try to figure out who had given it to him. It had to be someone who sat close to him. Margery, who sat in front of him, had already gone to get her jacket. She didn't act like someone who was waiting for a thank-you. Besides, she didn't ever seem to know any current events.

On his right side sat Kim, and on his left side sat Milt, but Milt was absent today, and it definitely wasn't Kim. She couldn't pass a note and sit on her hands at the same time. That only left the seat behind him.

Adam turned in his seat to look at Grayson. It was unlikely that Grayson would have written the note. Grayson was the best forward at Angell Elementary and he would make the team for sure. Plus, he was popular. Adam hardly ever played with anyone at recess, and Grayson was always surrounded by a group of boys playing soccer. So Adam didn't expect anything as he looked at Grayson.

Grayson returned Adam's look with a sigh of satisfaction. "I helped the math whiz." He grinned. "What do you think of that?"

Adam was flabbergasted. He smiled back, a little uncertainly. "Thanks."

"Go get your jackets, boys," said Ms. Werner gently. "You can talk and play outside."

Adam followed Grayson to the back of the room. Adam slipped on his green sweat-shirt jacket. It was ripped at the right elbow and had a splot of yellow tempera paint on the side where Nora had tried to make a picture of Fancy. Adam had caught her before she ruined it entirely. The yellow didn't show if he kept his left arm down by his side.

Adam zipped up his jacket and waited while the other children went out the classroom door and turned to go to the playground. Then Adam went out the door and headed for the boys' bathroom. He went in.

The bathroom was empty. Adam took off his jacket and let it fall on the floor. Then he rolled up each pant leg and pulled the tape from his legs. Some of his hairs stuck to the tape. Adam gritted his teeth and pulled quickly. When he had gone as far as he could, he let down his pant legs.

Now for the tricky part. He had to get the tape off his torso. It was important that no one should see him. Adam went into the first stall. He could manage to get the tape off the bottom half of his body without undressing completely. But he would have to take off his shirt to finish the job. He unbuttoned his shirt and slipped out of it; then he pulled off his T-shirt underneath. The hook for hanging things was broken off the inside of the stall door. Adam opened the door and went over to the sink. He folded his shirt and T-shirt and placed them neatly on the edge of the sink.

Adam looked down at his chest. There sure was a lot of tape there. He took the roll of tape out of his pocket. It was half gone. Maybe he should try to save some of the tape from his chest.

The bathroom door opened. Adam dashed into the first stall.

Someone turned on a faucet. Adam peeked under the stall door. The person was standing at the sink where Adam's shirts were. Adam saw a hand reach down for his jacket on the floor.

"Hey!" Adam burst out of the stall.

Grayson straightened up and leapt backward. He

knocked Adam's folded shirts into the sink, where the faucet was still running.

"My shirts!" Adam ran to the sink and grabbed the soggy mess.

Grayson stared. "Gee. I'm sorry." He looked from the wet shirts to Adam's bare chest. "You have tape on you."

Adam ripped the tape off his chest and neck and threw it in the trash. "My shirts."

Grayson looked at Adam strangely. "You had tape on your legs this morning, too. What's the tape for?"

"Just an experiment," said Adam. "My shirts are all wet."

"Experiment?"

"In communication." Adam picked up his green jacket. "Guess I'll just keep my jacket on this afternoon." He thought of trying to explain to Ms. Werner. His lips pursed.

"Listen, I wore a blue undershirt today. It can pass for a regular shirt. You want to wear it?" Grayson unbuttoned his shirt as he talked. He pulled off his undershirt and held it out to Adam.

"Thanks." Adam put on Grayson's undershirt. It went down to the middle of his thighs.

"You can give it back after soccer practice."

"Sure." Adam tugged at the undershirt hem to straighten it. "That makes two times you've helped me."

"That's right." A look of surprise slowly crossed Grayson's face. "And I'll do it more times. Lots more."

Adam stared at Grayson. It was amazing enough that Grayson had already rescued him twice. But the fact that Grayson, king of the soccer field, wanted to help Adam in the future was nothing short of a miracle. Adam cleared his throat. "How come?" he croaked.

" 'Cause you need it." Grayson nodded his head. "You need it, and I can do it."

"But how come you want to?"

Grayson stopped nodding his head. He sucked his top lip in under his bottom teeth. He looked around the bathroom. Then he said, " 'Cause then maybe you'll help me."

Adam got worried. "How could I help you?"

Grayson hesitated. Then he blurted out, "You could explain this math to me." His face went suddenly red. Adam remember the whispered "dumbo." He thought of how last year the fourth-grade teacher had given Grayson extra math work all the time. Grayson pressed his lips shut hard.

Then he said in a quiet voice, "All these fish and circles and arrows and things . . . I don't get it."

It was Adam's turn to nod. This was something he could do just fine. "All right," said Adam, "we'll help each other."

Grayson bobbed his head up and down. "Yeah. All right." He gave a small smile.

Adam smiled wide. Then he said it again, drawling it out over three syllables, "All right!"

CHAPTER 5

Soccer Practice

· ·

The soccer field was still muddy from yesterday's storm. Adam walked on tiptoe over to his assigned spot on the field, trying not to spatter mud up the sides of his new sneakers. He had begged his mother for those sneakers, saying that maybe with new sneakers he would run faster and kick harder and make the team. She told him to try to keep them clean and looking new for at least a week. That's why he hadn't worn them Monday or Tuesday. But he had to wear them today. He just had to. There wasn't much time left before the team would be chosen, and if the sneakers were going to help him, they had to do their job fast.

Coach Morrison blew his whistle, and someone kicked off. Adam watched the forwards converge on the ball. He saw William, from his class, fall and get up again, smeared with mud up the side of his jeans. Adam suddenly panicked. Everyone was playing hard today, running very close to each other in crowds. Adam hated crowding. If you were going to get hurt at soccer, it stood to reason that you'd probably get hurt the worst when everyone was crowding. Plus Adam's feet felt like they were anchored in cement today. His legs were still like boards. He knew he couldn't kick well right now. He prayed the ball wouldn't come his way.

That's when he felt a light blow on the back of his neck. He turned around just as an envelope made of folded lime-green construction paper fell onto the mud. It had ADAM printed in big letters across the front. Adam leaned over to pick up the envelope. His right foot slipped away from under him and he fell face forward. He wound up on his hands and knees, straddling the envelope. Mud squished up between his fingers.

The soccer ball rolled by with three boys in hot pursuit. Adam got up and looked around to see if the coach was watching. But Coach Morrison was running along the sidelines, keeping up with the ball, which by now was on the far side of the field.

Adam picked up the envelope and took out the

index card inside. Taped to it was a stem of a wilted plant with tiny leaves and a crumpled purple flower. And printed underneath it in blue crayon was the word *hi*.

Adam counted the leaves. Three. Poison ivy had three leaves. But Adam didn't think poison ivy had flowers. He wished he knew more about plants. His sister Catherine could identify every weed in sight. Her Girl Scout troop took the world of the outdoors seriously.

Adam quickly looked around, expecting to see Kim. She was the only person he could think of who might throw a plant in an envelope at him. But Kim was nowhere in sight. He stuffed the envelope, flower and all, in his jacket pocket and forgot about it.

For the rest of the scrimmage, Adam did his best to stay out of the way of the ball and, especially, of the boys who chased it. He was pretty successful, with the exception of once, when Grayson kicked the ball straight to him and Adam managed to kick it away before anyone jumped on him. He kicked it out of bounds.

When the scrimmage was over, Grayson came over to Adam. "You going home now?"

"Yeah," said Adam.

Grayson nodded. "You usually walk alone?"

"Yeah," said Adam.

Grayson fell in step beside him.

"Yo, Grayson!" Clifford came running up. "Let's go."

"Not today, Clifford." Grayson shoved his hands into his pants pockets. "Catch you later, okay?"

Clifford looked from Grayson to Adam. He rolled his eyes. "Later, sure." Then he ran off.

"What was in the envelope?" asked Grayson.

"How did you know about the envelope?"

Grayson kicked through the dead leaves on the sidewalk. "I saw Kim throw it. So what was in it?"

"A note, I guess," said Adam, not mentioning the flower. He felt his cheeks go hot. This morning Gordon had seen Kim talking to Adam before school, and now Grayson had seen Kim throw an envelope at him. People would make fun of him if she kept this up.

"She made you miss a good ball," said Grayson.

"Yeah, but I probably would have missed it any-how."

Grayson looked over at Adam and cocked his head to one side. "You know what you need?"

Adam thought about Coach Morrison's words the day before. He needed to pay more attention, keep his eyes on the ball, be ready for the next move. Oh, he knew what he needed all right. "No."

"You need practice."

"I come to practice."

"No," said Grayson. "Brainy kids like you have it all wrong."

Adam could feel it coming. He could hear Grayson's words in his head even before Grayson spoke them. Brainy kids shouldn't try out for soccer. Brainy kids should stick to their books. That's what Clifford had said to Adam last year after he didn't make the team. That's what Grayson would say now. "What have I got all wrong?" Adam asked, clenching his teeth.

Grayson kicked an acorn out of sight into the leaves. "You're coming at this all wrong."

Adam moved faster. "So what do you mean? Say it."

"You think about soccer too much. You stand there thinking, and when the ball comes your way, it's like you're not alert or something." Grayson looked at Adam. "That's not the way it happens. You've got to practice a lot. At recess. At home. All the time."

Adam nodded his head slowly. "I think I see what you mean. I have to actually play ball, not just think about it."

"Yeah," said Grayson. "You've got to kick that ball."

It sounded right. Adam thought of all the recesses he'd sat on the sidelines and coached the game in his head instead of joining in and playing. "But the official final tryout is Monday," said Adam. "And it's Wednesday already. There's no time for practice."

"Yeah, there is. My mom won't let me stay out late on a school night, but on Friday we can practice together. And Saturday and Sunday."

Adam got excited. "Yeah, you could teach me everything you know!"

Grayson nodded. "Mmm-hmmm. And after every time we practice, you can teach me some math." Grayson checked his watch. "I better go. My mom worries if I don't come straight home. Give me my undershirt."

Adam took off his jacket and pulled off the blue undershirt. He was cold, standing there bare-chested. He quickly zipped the jacket back on. "Thanks."

Grayson stuffed the shirt into his backpack and turned the corner. "Don't mention it." He started off, then suddenly turned and walked backward in giant steps without breaking his stride. "You know, you can't let Kim bug you."

Adam was confused. He thought of the beetle and the cricket. Bugs.

Grayson pointed his finger at Adam and shot it off like a gun. "Kim's after you."

Adam nodded. Kim Larkin was after him. He had to think about what that meant. But not now. Not with Grayson here. He needed time.

"Want some advice?"

Adam wasn't sure. This was man-to-man talk, and he felt like he didn't know what was going on. He looked at Grayson blankly.

"Ignore her," said Grayson. "That always works. Don't open envelopes she leaves around. And whatever you do, don't say anything to her."

"Hurry up," said Adam, standing in the doorway.

Nora splashed the water with both hands. "Look at all the bubbles."

"I need a bath, too. You've been in there for twenty minutes. The water must be cold already. Move it, would you?"

"Don't be so bossy."

"Look, Nora. You're five and I'm ten. I'm twice your age. Get out of the tub."

"No," said Nora. "*You're* five and *I'm* ten. No, you're ten and I'm eleven. No, you're eleven and I'm twelve. I'm as old as Catherine!"

"You're an idiot," said Adam.

"No," said Nora. "No, no, no." She climbed out of the tub. "We're both fourteen," she sang. She ran down the hall, dripping. "Yay!"

Adam watched his sister thoughtfully. He wondered if she had any chance at a normal life. Adam carefully closed the door all the way, emptied the tub, and undressed. Then he filled it again with the hottest water he could stand, and he got in. He sank down till his ears were under the water and his nose just poked out on top, and he listened.

"This water's soapy," grumped the voice Adam had come to recognize as Frankie's.

"His sister Nora took a bubble bath," said Gilbert. "The boy must not have let the tub empty all the way before he put in his own water."

"The jerk's dirty enough," said Frankie. "He should have taken a bubble bath himself. He falls too much at soccer. I can't wait till he fails the tryouts, and all this soccer nonsense stops."

Adam couldn't control himself any longer. "I heard you," he blurted out. Water filled his mouth and he sat up, spluttering and gagging.

He quickly slid back under the water. There was silence. "Don't pretend like you can't talk," shouted Adam under the water. He sat up, spluttering and gagging again.

There had to be a better way. Hey, obviously the freckles could hear him out of water, even if he couldn't hear them. So he could speak to them normally above water. But that way, they might say things to each other while his ears were out of the water, and he wouldn't know what they had said. Adam didn't want to miss anything, especially since Frankie had called him a jerk. They could say all sorts of things behind his back. He had to keep his ears underwater and his mouth out of the water at the same time.

He slid down and tipped his head back till his ears were underwater. "I know everything you say."

The freckles didn't answer.

"You think if you don't say anything, I'll forget about you. But I won't."

"It's possible," said Gilbert to Frankie.

"Nah," said Frankie.

"I hear you," shouted Adam. "The water is acting as a conductor."

"What's that, dear?" called Adam's mother from down the hall.

"Nothing," screamed Adam.

"I've been suspecting something for a while, anyway," said Gilbert, continuing to ignore Adam. "Just look at the way he scratches us when he does something bumbling. I bet he scratches because he feels us laughing."

"Laughing?" said Adam. "You laugh at me?"

"Sometimes you're as amusing as Nora," said Gilbert, finally addressing Adam directly.

"How do you know about Nora?" asked Adam.

"We live with you, kid," said Frankie. "And it's not always easy. You're so clumsy."

"And slow," said Gilbert.

"Yeah," said Frankie. "For once, Gil, you're making sense. The kid's a space cadet."

Adam couldn't take all the abuse. He sat up and pulled his knees out of the water so Gilbert and Frankie would get cold. His feelings were hurt. And he couldn't believe the betrayal. Here Gilbert and Frankie were his own freckles. In fact, Gilbert had been his favorite freckle until just now. And they were being disloyal to him. They laughed at him! Why, they should be working with him. They should help him.

That was it! His freckles should help him. Adam quickly lifted his left leg out of the water and inspected the calf all around. Then his right. He smiled at the freckles he had known all his life, literally dozens of them on each leg. He checked out both arms. They were peppered with freckles on every side. And, of course, there were all those freckles on his face. And the cluster of freckles on his right shoulder—the ones Frankie and Gilbert called snobby. And more on his back. Even on his bottom. And they were beautifully scattered. Adam had never thought of their even distribution as beautiful before. But now he realized it. His wonderful freckles faced every direction. Now the next question was more important than ever.

Adam slid under the water and lowered his knees. "Can all of you freckles see and talk?"

"Who wants to know?" asked Frankie angrily.

Adam lifted his knees out of the water again and held them there for ten seconds. Then he lowered them. "Okay, I have a deal for you."

"I don't appreciate getting cold like that," said Gilbert.

"Me either," said Frankie.

"Then answer me. Can all of you see and talk or not?"

"Of course we can," said Gilbert. "What do you think freckles are, perceptually deficient or something?"

Adam's excitement rose. Maybe it was true. Oh, if only it were true. "How come I don't hear the others talking? How come, when I put my ears under the water, I don't hear a whole crowd of freckles talking?"

"Most of us talk to our neighbors," said Gilbert.

"But Gilbert and me," said Frankie, "we're long-distance buddies. Knee-to-knee. So we shout to each other."

Adam thought about how Gilbert and Frankie had talked to each other during math class that morning. He felt confused for a moment. "Can you only talk to each other by way of a conductor?"

"Of course not," said Gilbert. "But it would appear that you can only hear us by way of a conductor. People have such obtuse ears; they miss most of the noise in the world."

"Well, my ears are not obtuse," said Adam. "They're sensitized. That's why I can hear you at all."

"Sensitized, are they? Well, then," said Gilbert, "if you listened more attentively, you could hear the others."

"Only they'd never talk to a half-wit like you," said Frankie.

"Hush," said Adam. He listened closely. He thought he heard a slight murmur through the water. Then he thought back to last night in the tub. His shoulder freckles talked last night. And the big freckle on the bottom of his left foot did, too. The evidence was pretty clear: They all talked, every one! Oh, glorious, fabulous, amazing, fantastic freckles! They talked, they saw, and they faced every direction. This was the best thing that had ever happened to Adam in his whole life. This was the thing that would give Adam a chance at soccer.

"All right, Gilbert." Adam spoke clearly, but softly, so that no one outside the bathroom would hear him this time. "Here's the deal. I want you all to help me play soccer better. You can watch out for the ball on all sides and tell me when it's coming. Then I'll kick it and I'll make the team."

"Not very likely," said Gilbert.

"You've got to be joking," said Frankie. "You have about as much chance as a snowball in hell."

"I'm dead serious. If you keep me alert to the ball, like Grayson says, I'll kick it. Grayson will teach me how to kick. All you have to do is tell me where the ball is, so I'm not looking one way when it's coming at me from the other way."

"We could do that, I suppose," said Gilbert slowly.

"Only what's in it for us?" said Frankie.

Adam sat up. What was in it for them? He slid under the water. "Well, I wouldn't fall as much 'cause I wouldn't get knocked into so much. You said you don't like it when I fall."

"I hate it when you fall," said Frankie, "but that's not enough."

Adam sat up again. He looked around the bathroom in desperation. His eyes lit on Catherine's body lotion on the back of the toilet. He slid under the water. "Catherine has body lotion. It makes your skin soft and . . . and kitteny."

"Kitteny?" said Gilbert.

"Kitteny?" said Frankie.

"Well, I don't know," said Adam. "That's what Catherine says. Anyway, it's very expensive. And if you help me, I'll rub it all over you."

"Wow," said Frankie. "I can be a kitten. I like the idea. I like it. Let's go for it, Gil."

"Hmmmm. The problem is," said Gilbert thoughtfully, "we can't all see the ball. We're covered up."

Adam thought of how chilly it was getting these days. But there seemed to be no choice. "All right, I'll wear shorts." Adam's teeth chattered at the thought. He slid under the water.

"We'll all be cold," said Frankie.

"I'll rub you with Catherine's kitten lotion when we get home every day," said Adam.

"And how will you be able to hear us?" said Gilbert.

"You're not going to play soccer underwater, are you?" said Frankie. He laughed at his own joke.

Adam furrowed his brows. This was a serious problem. He could hear the freckles in water and by way of the transparent tape. But he certainly couldn't put tape from every freckle on his body up to his ears. He'd be covered in tape! "Do all the freckles talk to you, Gilbert?"

"Of course. I am the leader, after all."

"What about those snotty beauty marks on his shoulder?" said Frankie.

"Well, we can overlook them. They're too small to count. All the significant freckles talk to me," said Gilbert.

"Then I can put tape to just you, and you can tell me everything they say. Is it a deal?"

"Tape?"

"Yeah. When I put tape from you to my ears, I can hear you talk," said Adam.

"So that's what happened in math class today," said Gilbert. "I wondered how he knew about the spider."

"He was eavesdropping," said Frankie.

"That's right." Gilbert hesitated. "We need a minute to talk it over. Please lift your head out of the water, boy."

Adam sat up. He was impatient and worried. His freckles had to agree. He had to make that team. He counted slowly to two hundred to pass the time. Adam's head had been out of the water for a few minutes, at least. It couldn't take very long for a group of freckles to talk over a simple idea like that. They had to be finished by now. He slid under the water and caught the tail end of the freckle meeting.

"Number 58, Humphrey?" said Gilbert.

"Aye."

"Number 59, Jethro?"

"Aye."

"All accounted for?"

There was a general murmuring of approval.

"All right, then," said Gilbert, "it's decided."

"Will you do it?" asked Adam, with his ears still underwater.

"Yes," said Gilbert. "It's a deal."

CHAPTER 6

Snakes

. . . .

On Thursday morning, Adam carefully ran a line of transparent tape from Gilbert up to his ear. Then he dressed in shorts and a short-sleeved shirt. He peeked at the thermometer mounted outside the bedroom window: 52 degrees. He shivered, even though he was still warm inside the house. He picked up the rest of the roll of tape and tucked it safely into his shorts pocket. That way, if the tape he had on got ruined during the day, he could put on new tape before soccer practice.

The trick now would be to get out of the house before his mother saw and made him change into clothes that covered his arms and legs. Adam went downstairs and slipped on his green sweat-shirt jacket and his backpack and tiptoed toward the front door. If he avoided the kitchen, he could avoid his mother.

Just then, smells wafted toward him from the kitchen. Adam lifted his nose and sniffed like a hound dog. Breakfast today was eggs and toast. There wasn't much Adam liked better than lightly scrambled eggs, soft but not gooey, and a piece of toast smeared thick with raspberry jam.

Adam was suddenly terrifically hungry. It would be a long wait till lunchtime. He didn't think he could make it. Besides, he realized with horror, all the makings for lunch were in the kitchen. If Adam went out the front door now, he would have to miss lunch, too. He thought of a nice, fat peanut butter and jelly sandwich, with an apple on the side. And maybe a small bag of potato chips. His mouth began to water.

Adam peeked into the kitchen. Catherine sat at the table with her Girl Scout sweat shirt on, munching toast. Nora was emptying her plate of eggs into Fancy's dish.

Adam's mother was nowhere in sight. Adam went into the kitchen with his finger up to his lips.

Catherine opened her mouth to speak, then saw his hush sign and shut her mouth. She eyed him suspiciously. "There's tape on you again," she whispered.

Adam popped a piece of bread into the toaster and laid out the makings for his lunch.

"And it's too cold for shorts," she whispered.

"I need shorts," Adam whispered back.

"I want to wear shorts, too," shouted Nora. "Mamma, I want to wear shorts, too. I want to wear my blue shorts with the sea horses all around the legs." Nora clattered up the back stairs singing.

Mamma came into the kitchen. She looked at Adam. "It's too cold for shorts. And you don't eat breakfast with your backpack on. Or your jacket. What's the matter with you this morning? Are you all right?"

"I'm fine, Mamma."

Mamma put her hand on her cheek and looked at Adam thoughtfully for a moment.

Adam stood tall and tried to look healthy. He gave her the toothiest smile he could manage. "I feel great."

Mamma shook her head. "Oh well, sit down and I'll make you some eggs, and then you can march right back upstairs and change into long pants. And I think I'll come up, too, and take your temperature, just to check. You look a little flushed." She bustled about making the eggs.

Adam quickly made a peanut butter and jelly sandwich, slipped it into a plastic bag, and put it into his lunch bag. Then he got a plum (there were no apples in the refrigerator today). Last, he added a granola bar (no bags of potato chips either—Mamma obviously needed to go shopping, but he didn't dare tell her and risk getting into any conversation that might lead to a discussion of his clothes). He put his backpack on the floor and sat down at the table. His jacket was still on.

Adam thought of going upstairs in shorts. Maybe he should just run upstairs and slip sweat pants on over his shorts. But if Mamma followed him upstairs, she would take his temperature, and who knew what might happen then. He was so excited about the day ahead, he might even be running a fever, and she'd never understand if he tried to explain.

It looked like shorts were it. The very idea made Adam put his hands in his jacket pockets for warmth. Just then his right hand closed over the envelope Kim had thrown at him on the soccer field yesterday. He took it out and shook the contents onto the table.

Catherine stared at the dried-up leaves and flower. "Why are you carrying around a dead violet?"

So that's what it was. Catherine had a future in horticulture, all right. "No reason." Adam swept the mess back into the envelope and shoved it into his pocket again.

Mamma put toast and a plate of fluffy eggs in front of Adam. "I've got to finish sewing a badge on Catherine's Girl Scout sash so she can wear it today. I'll be back in a few minutes."

"You're wearing a sash?" said Adam. "I heard you and your friend Sissy say seventh graders were too old to wear sashes."

"Our troop is going over to Burns Park Elementary today to help with the bridge ceremony for the Brownies that are flying up into a Junior troop," said Catherine. "We need the sashes for the ceremony."

"Why do they need a bridge if they're going to fly?" said Adam.

"Shut up," said Catherine.

"That's enough," said Mamma. "Adam, you make sure you change into jeans, young man. I'll see you upstairs in a few minutes, to take your temperature."

Adam gobbled his eggs agreeably, without saying a word. Once his mother was out of the kitchen, he stuffed the rest of the eggs into his mouth all at once and grabbed his backpack.

"You're not going to change?" Catherine whispered, amazement on her face.

Adam swallowed the eggs with difficulty. "I've got to wear shorts today." Adam jammed his lunch bag into the backpack. "Don't tell."

Catherine chewed her lip in doubt. "All right. This time. But you have to tell my why."

"I will later." Adam ran out of the house, pulling on his backpack as he ran. Good, cooperative sister. At least today she was being cooperative. Now if only his freckles would do the same.

"Your legs are all goose bumpy," whispered Kim. She smoothed her skirt at the knees. Adam saw her out of the corner of his eye.

Adam took out his silver crayon and carefully outlined the rocket ship he had drawn. He was just as careful not even to glance at his bare legs. They were cold. But at least his arms were covered by his sweat-shirt jacket. He had kept the jacket on all day. Anyway, Kim wasn't one to talk. She had on a skirt and her legs were bare. She had to be as cold as him, even if she didn't have goose bumps. Adam scratched his thumb.

"Did you look in the envelope?"

Adam thought about the envelope. A dead violet. Grayson had said Kim was after Adam. But somehow a dead violet didn't seem like what a girl would give a guy if she liked him. Actually, Adam had no idea what a girl would do if she liked him. No other girl had ever paid any attention to him. But the way Kim was acting didn't strike Adam as the way a girl *should* act if she liked him. Probably Kim wasn't after Adam in the way Grayson thought.

Besides, Kim still thought Adam had put the spider on her gum after she'd told him that she hated spiders. She might want to get even.

Adam took out his red crayon and colored the flames coming out of the rear of the rocket.

"I can see the tape on your left knee," said Kim.

Adam tried to pull his shorts legs down to cover his knees. It was impossible.

"What's it for?" Kim leaned across the aisle a little, and her whisper became so soft Adam could hardly hear it. "Are you going to do something amazing with it?"

Adam made the flames from the rocket fill half the page.

"If it's a secret, it's not working. Everyone can see it. Even Ms. Werner."

Adam thought about that. Ms. Werner hadn't told him not to wear tape. So she shouldn't get mad. She shouldn't do anything about it at all. He turned in his seat to look quickly at his teacher.

Ms. Werner was working with the third reading circle. While each circle met with Ms. Werner at the back of the room, the rest of the class was supposed to stay seated and do silent reading. Reading circles were the last thing on the schedule of lessons today. So by the time this circle ended, school would be over and Adam could run out to the soccer field for practice. He had gotten through the whole day without talking or looking at Kim at all. He was following Grayson's advice, and he wasn't about to give way now.

"And what if Ms. Werner examines your desk for tape? She might find any number of things." Kim hummed to herself tunelessly. "Any number of things."

Adam wondered what Kim meant. So what if Adam had tape in his desk? You couldn't get in trouble for having tape in your desk. Unless maybe Kim had put something else in his desk. Adam tried to remember if there had been anything unusual in his desk today. He'd opened it several times, but he hadn't looked around it carefully. He longed now to open it up and examine every corner. But that wouldn't be ignoring Kim. And he was supposed to ignore Kim. Maybe he could open it just a little to get another crayon. Then he could feel around for anything unusual, and Kim wouldn't even know he was doing it.

Unless the something unusual bit him.

But Kim couldn't have put anything alive in his desk again, could she? Something alive would have run out of the desk by now. Unless it was asleep. Or a slow mover, like that goofy lizard. Or some other reptile.

Adam thought back to yesterday morning and how Kim had suddenly appeared beside him on the way to school with that half-smushed cricket in her fist. She'd asked him then what animals he liked. She'd asked if he liked lizards. But first she had asked something else. Yeah. She had asked if he liked snakes.

And Adam had said he hated snakes.

Kim could have put a snake in Adam's desk. That would have been the perfect way to get even for the spider. A slow, sleepy, cold snake. With fangs.

Adam felt sweat beads form on his forehead. He didn't want a snake in his desk. But he couldn't leave it in there, either. He decided that quick action was needed.

Adam put both hands on the edge of the lid of his desk. He scooted his butt to the edge of his seat and swung his feet out into the aisle so he was ready. He snuck a glance at Kim. She was watching him with expectation all over her face. He counted slowly to three. Then he threw up the lid of his desk and jumped out into the aisle with a scream.

No snake popped out.

The desk lid slammed shut again with a *bang!*

"Adam!" Ms. Werner walked up the aisle. "Adam, what *is* the matter?"

Adam looked around helplessly. Kim was watching him with that new look of hers again. In fact, everyone was looking at him with that look—as though he were a total freak. Everyone except Ms. Werner. She looked angry. "I thought maybe there was something alive in my desk."

Ms. Werner's expression changed abruptly. She stepped back and looked warily at the desk from a safe distance. She spoke softly. "Another lizard, Adam?"

"I don't know."

"Spiders?" she whispered.

"I don't know."

"What do you think it was?" she whispered ever more softly. It seemed Ms. Werner was losing her voice entirely.

"Maybe a snake."

Ms. Werner backed down the aisle to the rear of the room, where the third reading group sat waiting for her with wide eyes. Instead of sitting down with them, she walked up the side aisle, glancing at Adam's desk every few steps, till she got to the front of the room. She opened her mouth to speak, but her voice wouldn't come. She smiled faintly and wrote on the blackboard in big letters: *Class dismissed.*

"But there's still ten minutes left of school," said Susanna.

Ms. Werner cleared her throat and managed a croaky voice. "You've all done well today. School's out early. Go home. Everyone except Adam."

The class broke into happy confusion, and Adam watched the others pack up their gear and pull on their jackets and tumble out the hall door. Adam sat silent at his desk, watching Ms. Werner. She stood behind her desk and appeared to be gazing out the window. The minute hand on the clock moved once. Then again. Time passed. The school bell rang. More time passed. Soccer practice had begun by now. Adam was late.

Ms. Werner recovered her normal voice. "Adam, please come up here." Ms. Werner sat down at her desk.

Adam walked to the front of the room and stood in front of Ms. Werner's desk.

"Did you put a snake in your desk?"

"No."

Ms. Werner bit her bottom lip. "Is there a snake in your desk?"

"I don't know." Adam looked down. "I don't think so. I was just worried."

"Are you afraid of snakes, Adam?"

"Yes."

"So am I. Do you want me to ask Mr. Peel to check your desk for you?"

Mr. Peel was the custodian. "No. I can do it myself."

"All right," said Ms. Werner. "You go check your desk while I wait here."

Adam walked back to his desk and lifted the lid. Everything in the desk looked normal. He sorted through the papers and books. There were several empty matchbooks and lots of crumpled silver foil from cigarette packs, the result of Adam and Gordon's treasure hunts on the way to school. At the very bottom of the desk under his math book was a tiny package wrapped in purple paper. Adam had never seen that package before. He slipped it into his shorts pocket.

He walked back up the aisle to Ms. Werner's desk.

"No snakes?"

"No snakes."

"Was there anything alive in the desk?"

"No."

"Anything strange at all?"

Adam decided not to mention the purple package. It might have something in it that would get him in trouble. He shrugged his shoulders.

"Why did you think there was something in your desk?"

Adam shifted from one foot to the other. "Just a feeling."

Ms. Werner patted her hair in worry. "Adam, there's tape on your knee again. Do you want to tell me why you're wearing tape?"

Adam thought about it. No, he was pretty sure he didn't want to tell Ms. Werner that. He shrugged again.

Ms. Werner shook her head sadly. "Will you tell me why you wore shorts to school today?"

"I thought I'd do better at soccer practice."

"Oh." Ms. Werner looked slightly relieved. "But aren't you a little cold?"

"A little."

"Don't you think you could do just as well in a comfortable pair of trousers?"

"Not today." Adam looked at the disappointment on Ms. Werner's face. She was a nice teacher. He hated to disappoint her. "But tomorrow there's no practice, so I can wear long pants." He watched her face light up. "But Monday is the final tryouts, so I'll have to wear shorts again." Her face fell.

"And after that?"

After that Adam would either be on the team, if a miracle happened, or off. Either way, shorts wouldn't be needed. "After that I can wear long pants every day."

"Good," said Ms. Werner, standing up. "I can see you've been worried about this soccer business. Once the tryouts are over I expect all your strange behavior will stop." She smiled. "That's all settled, then."

Adam liked Ms. Werner. She was worried about him. Well, pretty soon he *would* act normal again. For now, he had to run. Coach Morrison would be mad at him as it was. "Can I go?"

"Of course."

Adam ripped off his sweat-shirt jacket and ran back to his desk to grab his backpack.

"Adam, you've got on short sleeves! Why are you taking your jacket off?"

"It'll make me play soccer better," Adam said over his shoulder. He stopped briefly at the doorway and gave a small wave. "Thanks, Ms. Werner."

She sank into her desk chair with a sigh and waved back.

Adam ran down the corridor as fast as he could and out to the soccer field.

CHAPTER 7

Freckles in Action

"From the left, look!" shouted Gilbert.

Adam spun to the left. The soccer ball flew right at him. He kicked it away as hard as he could. It was a good kick. Only it went toward his own side's goal. He would have to learn how to react fast and still kick the ball in the right direction. Next time. He looked over at Coach Morrison. The coach was shouting to a forward from the sidelines. He wasn't paying any attention to Adam. But next time the ball came Adam's way, he would kick it in the right direction, and Coach Morrison would see.

Adam waited patiently in his assigned area. He played defense, and he knew he wasn't supposed to move far from his area. He ran in place to keep warm. His legs and arms were freezing.

"Behind," said Gilbert, "coming up from the right."

Adam turned around. A group of boys was advancing on him with the ball in their midst. There was an open space on his side. Maybe he could get at the ball. If only no one would hurt him. Adam couldn't stand the idea of being trampled. He gritted his teeth and tried to enter the group. He got shoved aside immediately.

But he didn't fall. At least he didn't fall.

The ball was up at the other end of the field now. Maybe his side would make a goal. Adam relaxed for a moment and looked off toward his classroom window. He thought about the snake he'd feared was in his desk. He felt stupid at the memory.

"Turn around *now*," ordered Gilbert.

Adam turned around. A forward from the side was dribbling the ball along fast, with a group of boys rushing up behind him. The forward looked across the defense and headed toward Adam's side. He obviously thought Adam would be easy to get past. Adam felt a momentary sag: He *was* easy to get past.

The forward was William. Adam knew William. William was just an ordinary kid. Adam could try to block him. He could try, at least.

As if Gilbert had read Adam's mind, he called

out, "Get in there, boy! Give him a run for his money!"

Adam ran straight at William shouting, "Charge!"

William looked up, startled. His jaw hung open.

Adam kicked the ball right through William's legs to a forward from his own team. It was Clifford. Adam had to admit that Clifford was good, even if Clifford was mean to him. Clifford took off with the ball, down the field. The other forwards ran close to him.

Adam looked around to see if anyone had noticed his kick. Sure enough, Coach Morrison was looking at him with a puzzled expression. Adam smiled at the coach. The coach hesitated, then he smiled back.

The scrimmage was going well. Adam was amazed by his freckles in action. For a moment he forgot how cold he was.

"All right," said Catherine, shutting the bedroom door and turning off the light. "You've been weird for two days now. Ever since the lightning. What's going on?"

Adam didn't stir. If he lay very, very still, she might think he was asleep like Nora.

"You don't fool me." Catherine went to Adam's bureau. "I'm going to steal all your Coke bottle caps." She opened the top drawer.

Adam sat up in bed. "Stop!"

"Aha!" Catherine looked in the drawer. "What junk!" She reached her hand in and stirred through the mess.

Adam jumped out of bed, ran to the bureau, and shoved the drawer shut, barely allowing Catherine time to pull her hand back.

"What's this?" Catherine held up the tiny purple package.

"I don't know," said Adam.

"You don't know? You have a package in your drawer and you don't know what it is? I don't believe you."

Adam reached for the package. Catherine held it over her head.

"Who's it for?" said Catherine.

"Me, I think."

"Someone gave it to you?" Catherine looked at Adam as though he was crazy. "Who gave it to you?"

"A kid in my class."

"Why don't you open it?"

"I was planning to," said Adam. And he had been. When he was undressing for his bath, he found the forgotten package in his pocket. He planned to open it after his bath. But Nora was still awake when Adam came into the bedroom, so he went straight to bed.

Catherine ran to Adam's bed now and sat on the foot of it. "Come on." She held out the package to him. "Open it."

Adam took the package and slid between the sheets. He ripped open the paper. Gum fell onto his lap. A half piece of purple bubble gum.

Catherine frowned. "Half a piece? Who'd give you half a piece of gum?"

Adam shrugged.

"Purple gum in purple paper," said Catherine. "A girl."

Adam shrugged.

"And this morning you had a dead violet in an envelope."

Adam shrugged.

"This girl's pretty obsessed with you, huh?"

Adam shrugged again.

"You're kind of young for that sort of thing."

Adam's shoulders were tired from shrugging. He looked at his sister in silence.

"Give me half."

Adam bit the gum in half, and they sat on his bed chewing.

"So is this girl the reason you've been putting tape all over yourself?"

"Nope."

"Well, you promised you'd tell. So tell."

"The tape lets me hear my freckles talk."

Catherine stared at Adam. "Your freckles? Did you say your freckles?"

"They're all over me, see?" Adam pulled up his pajama sleeves and showed Catherine the freckles on both arms.

"I *know* you have freckles all over you, Adam. I'm your sister!" Catherine looked bewildered.

Adam pulled up his pajama legs and pointed. "And this one's the leader. His name is Gilbert."

Catherine nodded up and down slowly, with a sick look on her face. "You named a freckle?"

"He already had a name. And this one over here, his name is Frankie."

"Adam," Catherine said, taking a gulp. "Adam, the doctor said you were going to be all right. But, well, maybe he was just being, well . . . I don't know . . . doctors can lie."

"You don't understand. They help me at soccer. We're sort of a team ourselves."

"Your freckles help you at soccer?"

"Sure. They tell me when the ball is coming up from behind. Then I turn around quick and kick like crazy."

Catherine reached out a hand and felt Adam's forehead.

Adam brushed her hand away. "Today I kicked the ball and it went in the right direction. I mean, it didn't go in the goal or anything. It wasn't even an assist. And the other side got it back fast. But it was a good kick. I kicked it right, Catherine. I did it! Me and my freckles, we did it!"

Catherine screwed up her lips and spoke very slowly. "Adam, why did you wear shorts and a short-sleeved shirt to school today?"

"Well, for the freckles, of course."

"For the freckles?" said Catherine, her face blank.

"They can't see through cloth."

"They can't see through cloth," repeated Catherine, her face showing worry. "If they can talk, why can't they see through cloth?"

"You can talk, but you can't see through cloth."

"I'm not a freckle."

"Come on, Catherine. Don't act dense. Seeing and talking have nothing to do with each other."

"Adam, you're the one who thinks his freckles talk, and you're calling me dense? Adam . . ." Catherine sighed. "Adam, you've got problems."

"I made a great kick today; didn't you hear me? I want to get on that team, Catherine."

Catherine nodded sympathetically. "It's the strain, Adam. You're cracking under the strain."

"I am not cracking."

"You are." Catherine spoke emphatically. "I know you felt bad when you didn't make the team last year. And I was sorry for you when I saw you reading all those newspaper articles last summer about the World Cup, drooling over Italy's team and Brazil's team. You were pathetic."

"Argentina, not Brazil."

"Who cares?" said Catherine. "It's all just a stupid game."

"You don't understand," said Adam. "Soccer is anything but stupid. It's a game of strategy. You have to plan every move."

"Look at you. You're acting like some sports maniac. What happened to my brainy brother? You're irrational these days. You rave like a lunatic about freckles with names."

Nora rolled over and moaned in her sleep.

Adam whispered, "Do you want to hear them talk for yourself? I can put tape from Gilbert to your ear."

"I don't want to be taped to your knee."

"Or I can put Gilbert in the tub, and you can stick your head underwater and listen."

Catherine let out a slow whistle. "You're totally berserk."

"Okay," said Adam. He stood up fast and hit his head on the top bunk. "Ouch!" He ran to his drawer. "Okay, I'll prove it to you." He rolled up his pajama legs as he talked. Then he took out the tape and stuck one end on Gilbert and ran it up to his ear. "All right, Catherine," he said with his back to her, "all right. You do something, and my freckles will tell me what you did."

Catherine was silent behind Adam's back.

"Did you do something? Okay, now, Gilbert, what did she do?" Adam listened.

Nothing.

"Gilbert," he said. "Gilbert, wake up. What's my sister doing?"

Nothing.

"Adam, you're scaring me," said Catherine. "I'm going to get Mamma if you don't get back in bed right now."

"Gilbert!" Adam pinched his knee. "Gilbert, answer me!"

"We're not a troop of trained dogs," said Gilbert. "We don't appreciate being ordered around. And, for goodness' sake, cease that obnoxious pinching."

"Sorry," said Adam.

"It's okay, Adam," said Catherine. "Just get in bed quietly."

"I didn't say sorry to *you*," said Adam. "I said sorry to Gilbert. *Sorry*, Gilbert."

"Show the proper respect," said Gilbert.

"I said sorry. What's she doing, anyway?"

"You broke your promise," said Gilbert.

"What? What are you talking about?" said Adam.

"I didn't say anything," said Catherine.

"I'm *not* talking to you, Catherine. Could you please shut up? Gilbert, what are you talking about?" said Adam.

"You said you'd put that feline body lotion on us if we assisted you. Well, we did our part, and you didn't."

"I had to rush through the bath tonight. I swear. Mamma's been worried about me and she said I had to go to bed early." Adam rubbed his knee gently. "I'm sorry. Please help me now. I'll put the feline lotion on you tomorrow."

"Feline lotion?" said Catherine in a yelp. "Don't you even think of putting any feline lotion or canine lotion or any other kind of lotion on me."

"I'm not talking to *you*," said Adam. "Gilbert, Gilbert, please tell me what my sister's doing."

"She's creeping up behind you."

"You're creeping up behind me," said Adam, twirling around and coming face-to-face with Catherine. "See! I knew what you were doing."

"You peeked," said Catherine.

"I did not."

"You heard me."

"Did not."

"You guessed."

"Did not."

"What's all this talk about feline lotion?"

"Nothing."

Catherine took Adam by the arm and pulled him back to his bed. "Sit down." Adam sat on the bed. Catherine sat beside him. She spoke half to herself. "Just like I said: totally berserk."

"I am not berserk."

"Your brain was fried, Adam. Oh, it's been a long time coming. You've been degenerating since last year. But the lightning really topped it off." Catherine nodded.

Adam scratched his knee. "No."

"And some girl gives you presents of half pieces of gum. Purple gum. And dead flowers. She must be crazy, too."

Adam shook his head. "She is not."

"Aha! Who is it, then?"

"I don't know for sure. So I'm not telling."

"Listen, Adam, if you know what's good for you, you won't tell anyone about the freckles, either. Believe me, they'll lock you up."

Adam looked at Catherine solemnly. She was probably right.

"And they'll throw away the key."

Adam and Catherine sat in silence, chewing purple bubble gum as the night got darker and darker.

CHAPTER 8

Getting Started

. . . .

When Adam got to school on Friday, he examined the inside of his desk thoroughly. There was nothing unusual in it. Still, all day long Adam was on guard. He worried about the gum that Kim had given him yesterday. If it had been poisoned, he would have died by now. He hadn't thought about that at the time. If it was some part of a terrible trick, he hadn't yet discovered what. His teeth hadn't turned purple; his hair hadn't fallen out; his tongue hadn't swollen to twice its normal size.

Maybe the gum wasn't a trick. That would mean that Kim had done something nice for him.

And maybe Kim knew the difference between poison ivy and violets. Maybe the dried-up plant in the envelope on the soccer field was supposed to be something nice, too.

Even the lizard could have been something nice.

Maybe Kim was being nice to Adam all along.

Maybe Grayson was right.

Adam looked over at Kim, searching for some sign of whether or not she really liked him.

But Kim gave no sign. She didn't speak to him, and he didn't speak to her, all day long. Once he caught her looking at him with that odd, awestruck expression on her face, but only once.

And once he thought about thanking her for the gum. Then he decided not to. There was no point in ruining perfectly good silence.

The school day slipped away peacefully.

There was no soccer practice after school. Coach Morrison liked Friday to be the beginning of his weekend, so he never held practice on Friday. That meant no more soccer stress (as Catherine called it) until Monday. But Monday was major stress: Monday would be the official and final soccer-team tryout.

Adam and Grayson walked together to Grayson's house after school, and the work began. They agreed to spend an hour on soccer and an hour on math.

Grayson had already prepared for the soccer practice. He had set up a series of truck tires in his driveway, and Grayson had a long, long driveway. There were sixteen tires in various spots.

"Where did all these tires come from?"

"My dad picks them up for me. I use them for practice all the time."

"How?" said Adam.

"You'll see. I'm going to run. Take your left hand and hold on to the back of my shirt and run behind me."

Adam looked around. "Where's the ball?"

"No ball today. We'll get to that tomorrow." Grayson spoke confidently.

Adam leaned over and started to roll up his pant legs so that his freckles could see.

Grayson tapped Adam on the shoulder. "What are you doing?"

"I do better when my legs can . . ." Adam hesitated; then he finished, "when they can breathe."

Grayson gave a small, awkward smile. Then his face got serious. "You don't need breathing legs. Just listen to me and do what I say. Roll down your pant legs, okay? Try it my way." Grayson sucked his top lip inside his bottom teeth.

Adam had come to recognize Grayson's sucking on his top lip as a sign of nervousness. Grayson was worried. Grayson thought Adam was a nut, just like

Catherine said. Adam had better be careful. If Grayson got even a hint of what was going on with Adam's freckles, he might dump this whole helping thing, just like that. And then Adam would be on his own again.

Adam didn't want to be on his own again. He liked Grayson. Besides, Grayson was the best soccer player Adam had ever seen in action. If Adam could learn to play like Grayson . . . Well, that was too much to ask. But maybe he could learn something. Some small thing. Adam rolled down his pant legs.

"Good," said Grayson with relief. "Now just hold on and run." He held out the edge of the back of his shirt.

Adam looked at the shirt; then he looked at Grayson's face. "But if I hold on to you, I'll trip on your heels."

"That's the point. You've got to learn to run close to me without getting tripped up. Take hold."

Adam took the edge of Grayson's shirt.

"Okay," said Grayson, "let's go."

Grayson dashed around the tires, going in and out, sometimes in full circles. Adam tripped on Grayson's heels. He learned quickly to run slightly to the side of Grayson instead of directly behind. He was surprised to find that keeping up with Gray-

son was no problem. Adam was pretty fast when he wasn't worried about getting crushed. The problem now was that Adam tripped over his own feet. But pretty soon he got the hang of it and hardly stumbled at all.

"You're getting there." Grayson stopped and panted. "The running's getting better."

Adam went over and leaned with his back on the garage. In spite of the cold, they were both sweating.

Grayson checked his watch. "Twenty minutes gone. Time for the second phase." He looked Adam up and down. "You're short."

This was news? Adam had been one of the shortest kids in his class, boys and girls included, ever since kindergarten. His father told him to be patient, wait till adolescence. Then he would hit a growth spurt and shoot up. But Adam didn't count on it. He figured he would probably be the shortest guy around all his life. And that would be okay, so long as it didn't stop him from doing things. He looked back at Grayson. "I know."

"That helps. The other team will think you're weak. You'll fool them."

Adam grinned. "That's something I never thought about. I've got the surprise element on my side."

"You've got to stop standing up straight as you run, though. That's the reason you fall so easy." Grayson hunched over. "Do like this, and you'll feel the difference."

Adam hunched over and ran in a little circle. "I see. The balance is all different. It's a question of center of gravity."

Grayson looked at Adam doubtfully. "I don't know."

"Sure you do. Your center of gravity is the point in your body that divides you into two parts of equal weight. When you hunch over like this, you move your center of gravity forward. It feels better for running."

"Yeah," said Grayson. "And if you're running standing tall and you get hit, you fall. But if you're running curled over and you get hit, you can keep moving."

"I get it," said Adam. "Your balance will be better, and you'll keep your momentum."

"You use big words," said Grayson.

Adam thought about Frankie accusing Gilbert of using fancy words. He smiled half to himself. "They mean the same thing you're saying. Different words, but the same idea."

"Okay," said Grayson. "So run curled over. Start around the tires. I'll run at you from different sides and bang into you. Not hard. And you try to keep on going in the same direction. Go!"

Adam ran and Grayson bumped into him. Over and over again, Adam fell on the hard concrete driveway. Once. Twice. He curled over more and held his own for a while. Then he fell again.

"Wait," said Grayson. "Something's not right. You're not taking the hit in the right way. Here, you slam into me." Grayson began running slowly, patting his left upper arm. "Right here. Come on."

Adam galloped sideways and slammed into Grayson's arm.

Grayson swayed with the blow and kept running. "See what I mean?"

"I think so," said Adam. "You're loose."

"That's it," said Grayson. "Think loose."

So Adam ran, thinking loose. And Grayson ran into him. And Adam let his body sway and kept on running. And Grayson kept on banging into him. And Adam stayed up and running.

"Yeah," said Grayson. He stopped again, with his hands on his hips, panting. "You're a fast learner."

"Thanks." Adam leaned forward, his hands on his knees, exhausted.

Grayson checked his watch and gave a satisfied smile. "The last thing to learn today is how to dodge.

I'll run at you, and you try to get past me without bumping into me."

Adam nodded. "That's all there is to it?"

Grayson laughed. "Dodging is tough. I'll block you every step of the way." Grayson crossed his arms at his chest. "Think you can get past me?"

Adam thought back to all the times he'd sat on the sidelines and watched Grayson do his famous fake-outs. "Sure."

Grayson grinned. "How?"

"You'll see. Stand back."

Grayson moved back several feet, and Adam ran toward his left. As Grayson lunged to the left, Adam dodged to the right, but he did it too early. Grayson shifted sides, too. Grayson felt like a brick wall as Adam slammed into him.

"You okay?" said Grayson.

"Yeah," said Adam. "I almost made it past you."

"I know," said Grayson. "You fooled me. You just did it a little too early. How'd you learn that?"

"I watch you when I'm on the sidelines."

"You watch me?" Grayson looked pleased. "Come on," he said, walking backward and beckoning Adam forward. "Come on and try me."

Adam raced toward Grayson's left. Grayson took the bait and lunged to the right at the last minute.

105

But this time, instead of dodging, Adam kept going. Right past Grayson.

"All right!" shouted Grayson. "Again."

And they went at it again and again and again. Dodging came easy to Adam. He was light on his feet and he shifted directions much faster than Grayson.

"That's it for today. You did better than I expected. You're okay for a brain."

"Grayson, who taught you all this stuff?"

"I don't know. I sort of picked it up playing. And my dad gives me some pointers. He's better than Coach Morrison." Grayson led Adam into the house. "Want some lemonade?"

"Sure," said Adam. "Then we can start on math."

Grayson laughed apologetically. "I won't be as fast at catching on in math as you are at soccer."

"Sure you will," said Adam.

"Ha! Famous last words from the brain." Grayson sucked his top lip inside his bottom teeth and glanced up at Adam briefly.

"You can do it, Grayson," said Adam. "You know what you're doing."

Grayson poured them both lemonade.

Adam took a sip. "I watch you on the field sometimes. You've got some good plays worked out. You use good strategies. Anyone who can figure out soccer plays like that can do math."

Grayson stirred his lemonade, keeping his eyes on the swirling liquid. "Soccer isn't math." He kept on stirring. "I'm just not good at this math thing. I don't understand any of it."

"That's not true. The whole idea of center of gravity is a math-type idea. And you understand it. You're the one who figured out that it was better to curl over when you run. You were doing the right thing."

"That's common sense," said Grayson, "not math."

"Math is common sense, too," said Adam, "if you let yourself look at it that way. The problems are no harder. You just have to let yourself think about it as though it were an ordinary thing—as though it were soccer."

"As though math were soccer!" Grayson smiled sheepishly. "You're funny, you know."

"Come on," said Adam. "Let's start."

So they spent the next hour drawing circles full of fish and practicing the times tables. Once Grayson saw the connection between the two, he knew how to figure out which school of fish Goldie would eat. It wasn't so hard for him. The real problem was that Grayson didn't know his times tables.

"So work on them," said Adam.

"They're not easy. I can't figure them out as fast as you."

"I don't figure them out," said Adam. "I memorized them. Everybody does. You have to."

"I never did," said Grayson.

"I can see that," said Adam. "So that's your homework for tonight. You memorize the tables up to six, and I'll give you a quiz in the morning."

"Then I'll make a soccer test," said Grayson. "And you'll take it."

Adam laughed. "You're on."

That night in the tub Adam scrubbed himself well. Then he slid down till his ears were underwater. "Ready, guys?" he said.

"Are you addressing us?" said Gilbert.

"Yeah," said Adam.

"Ready for what?" asked Gilbert.

"You'll see." Adam held his legs up out of the water and reached for Catherine's body lotion, which he had set on the edge of the tub in preparation. He put a dab of the thick, pale green liquid on each knee. Then he quickly rubbed it into his skin.

He held his legs out of the water for a couple of minutes, until his thighs began to ache from the strain. Then he lowered them into the water and listened.

He heard definite purring.

"You like it, don't you?" said Adam.

"Like it? This is the cat's meow," said Frankie. "Oooeee. The life of luxury."

"Well, you are a man of your word, after all," said Gilbert. "This is a most satisfying experience. Yes, indeed."

Satisfying. Yeah, thought Adam. It had been a truly satisfying day all around.

CHAPTER 9

Weekend Work

· ·

"Put your foot on top of the ball, like this." Grayson put his right foot on top of the soccer ball. "Hop on your other foot and move the ball forward and back and sideways under your right foot." He hopped around, moving the soccer ball continually under his right foot. He turned in a circle, with the ball sticking under his foot as though it were glued there.

Adam stood in the cold Saturday morning air and shivered, even though he was warmly dressed in jeans and a sweat shirt under his jacket. Last night, when he went to bed, he felt terrific. Grayson was a nice person. They laughed together. And it seemed that Adam was learning everything about soccer fast. Then Gilbert had promised Adam in the tub that all his freckles would stand by him at

Monday's tryouts. Between the freckles and Grayson, things looked good. It seemed he had a chance at getting on the team. But this morning everything looked different. His freckles were hidden and silent under his clothes, and, as Adam watched Grayson, he felt like his old clumsy self again. Grayson moved quickly with the ball. He was graceful and smooth. He was agile. Adam could never be that way.

"Hey, wake up," Grayson called. "You've got my best ball. Try it."

Adam looked down at the soccer ball he held wedged between his feet. Well, he was here. He might as well try. He stood on his left foot and put his right on top of the ball and hopped. The ball rolled away. Adam looked up.

Grayson smiled and hopped around him, keeping his ball moving with him under his right foot. "Try again."

Adam hopped. The ball rolled away. Adam slumped his shoulders and sighed.

"Giving up already?" Grayson stopped hopping and stood right in front of Adam. "You have to keep at it." He lifted his chin in a challenge. Then he hopped away with his ball.

Adam set his own chin and hopped again. Every time the ball rolled away, Adam got it back and hopped some more. He counted to himself. This time he kept the ball under his foot for three seconds before it rolled away. He worked up to ten seconds. It was progress of a sort. Sure. He hopped and looked up at Grayson. The ball rolled away.

"Okay, now keep on like that, but don't look at the ball. Look at me."

"What?" Adam ran after the ball and put it back under his foot. "If I look at you, I'll never be able to do it."

"Yes, you will. You have to." Grayson pointed at the ball. "My dad says there are two rules about the ball. One: If you don't have it, keep your eyes on it and get it. Two: If you have it, let your feet keep track of it and keep your eyes on where you're going and get a goal." Grayson hopped off toward the line of five tires he had set up. "Follow me." He hopped in and out, around the tires.

Adam hopped along, losing the ball immediately. He got it back and hopped some more. It took time to work back up to ten seconds. Then he made it to fifteen. Then twenty. Then twenty-three.

Grayson stopped and looked at his watch. "Wow! We've been working thirty-five minutes already. An hour isn't very long for this sort of thing." He looked worried. "Okay, I'm going to show you only two things this morning, but you're going to have to practice them all afternoon at home by yourself."

"I don't have a ball."

"You can take the one you're using. It's a great ball. It's my favorite. And you can start working on your mom to buy you one."

Adam didn't think he could do any of this alone. He needed Grayson's help. "Maybe we could practice together this afternoon, too. Why not?"

Grayson shook his head. "My mom's taking me shopping today. All my warm clothes are too small." Grayson went over to the tires and arranged them a little farther apart. "Now for dribbling." He stood in front of Adam and kicked the ball back and forth between his feet, while staying in place. "You've got to keep the ball under you. Kick it with the inside of your feet. When you get good at it, travel. First up and down the driveway. Then in and out of the tires."

Adam looked down at the ball and kicked it between his feet.

"Eyes up," shouted Grayson. "Never look at the ball once you've got it. Remember?" He dribbled around the tires.

Adam fixed his eyes on Grayson and dribbled the ball between his feet. After a while, he started to move with it. The ball kept flying away. Adam had to learn not to kick too hard. Just hard enough to get the ball to the other foot in the same amount of time it took that foot to make a running step. Adam dribbled up and down the driveway. Then he went through the tires.

"Let's go on the sidewalk," said Grayson. He headed off, dribbling toward South University Avenue.

Adam dribbled after him. The ball flew into the street and under a parked laundry truck. By the time Adam fished it out, Grayson was already at the corner. Adam dribbled after him as fast as he could. But the faster he went, the less control he had. The ball whizzed out into the street, and a passing car beeped at Adam. Adam waited for the ball to roll back to the gutter. He picked it up and turned to follow Grayson, but Grayson was already back beside him.

"We need a field, really," Grayson said. "Tomorrow let's meet at school."

"Okay," said Adam.

"Yo, Grayson!" Clifford came up the sidewalk on his skateboard. He had on a helmet, kneepads, and thick, rough-looking gloves like the kind Adam's dad wore in the garden. He saw Adam look him up and down, and he shrugged. "My mother's got this safety thing."

Adam shrugged back.

Clifford looked at Grayson. "I'm going over to the Bagel Factory. Want to come?"

Grayson hesitated. He opened his mouth and looked at Adam. But he didn't say anything.

Adam felt the heat rise in his cheeks. Grayson had already given him enough time. "I guess I should get going anyway," said Adam. He put Grayson's favorite ball under his right foot and hopped around Clifford.

Clifford turned in a circle. "Hey, that's pretty good," he said, keeping his eyes on the ball. "When did you learn to do that?"

Adam closed his lips in determination and hopped around Clifford a second time.

"I can't come right now," said Grayson. "We're sort of busy."

Clifford looked at Grayson as though he were nuts. "You're busy with Adam?"

"Yeah." Grayson dribbled the ball between his feet. "Another time, okay?"

Clifford made a clicking noise with his mouth. Then he skated off, calling over his shoulder, "If you change your mind, I'll be there."

Adam moved beside Grayson. "If you want to go—"

"He's not a jerk," said Grayson quickly, cutting Adam off, "even if he acts jerky sometimes. If you're not good at soccer, he has trouble liking you." Grayson sucked on his top lip. "I'm not saying this right."

"It's okay," said Adam. "I don't really care."

Grayson looked around, then back at Adam. "You were getting really good at dribbling, you know." He checked his watch. "Test time." He dribbled back to the driveway.

For the next ten minutes, Adam was tested on running while holding on to Grayson's shirt, on staying on course even when Grayson bumped into him, and on getting past Grayson's block. He got a point off for every time he tripped. He got a point off for every time he went off course. He got a point off if it took him longer than ten seconds to get past Grayson's block.

"Your final score is minus twelve."

"Yuck." Adam scratched his head. "I never got a minus twelve on anything before."

"So count it off from a hundred. Eighty-eight. Not too bad."

Adam smiled. "I know you can subtract. Let's go test your multiplication."

Grayson and Adam went into the house, and Grayson rattled off the times tables for Adam. All the way through the sixes. Then Adam asked him problems at random. "Five times six?"

"Thirty."

"Three times nine?"

"Twenty-seven."

"Seven times six?"

"Hey, that's the sevens table. I haven't memorized that yet."

"But you know it." Adam unfolded the sheet of paper that he had written all the tables on last night. He smoothed it out. "What's three times four and four times three?"

"They're both twelve."

"What's four times six and six times four?"

"They're both twenty-four."

"What's five times nine?"

"Forty-five."

"Okay, now look at this table. What's nine times five?"

"Forty-five." Grayson pulled the sheet of paper toward him. He moved his finger around. "Oh, I get it. It's the same answer, no matter which one comes first."

"That's right," said Adam. "So what's seven times six?"

Grayson hesitated.

"The same as six times seven," said Adam softly.

"Forty-two." Grayson grinned. "That means I know most of the tables for seven, eight, nine, and ten already."

"Uh-huh. And by tomorrow, you'll know the rest 'cause that's your homework."

Grayson groaned. But he folded the sheet of times tables and put it into his pocket.

"Now for the problems. If there are three really great forwards on the soccer team, and they each make eight goals, how many goals does the team make?"

"That depends on whether or not the other players make any goals."

Adam smiled. "Let's say they don't."

"Twenty-four."

"Now, let's say there's a soccer game with new rules. Only three forwards on each team can score goals, and they all have to score the same number of goals or the team loses. Understand?"

Grayson made a gooney face. "Crazy rules, but I got them."

"Good," said Adam. "Now one team gets eleven points, and the other team gets nine. Which team wins?"

"The one that gets eleven can't win. But the one that gets nine might or might not."

Adam was confused. "Why not?"

" 'Cause it depends on whether the nine points were made equally by the three forwards or not."

"Let's say they were," Adam said.

"Okay, then the team with nine points wins," said Grayson.

"That's right. Now explain to me why the team with eleven points couldn't win."

Grayson smiled. " 'Cause the forwards on the better team were too aggressive and they didn't stay even with each other on getting goals."

"Right," said Adam. "Eleven doesn't go into three equal groups, but nine does. So the forwards on the team with eleven points didn't all make the same number of goals, but the forwards on the team with nine did."

"This is a really stupid soccer game, you know?"

Adam laughed. "And it's just like Goldie."

"You're right. Goldie is stupid. She should just gobble up all the fish she finds."

"Only then it wouldn't be math class."

Grayson and Adam laughed together.

CHAPTER 10

Daisies

Sunday lunch was wonderful. Roast chicken, peas, salad, and coconut custard pie. It was all fabulous except for the chicken, peas, and salad. Adam wished every meal could be that good. He always looked forward to Sunday lunch. Mamma had made this one specially good because Daddy had announced last night that he had to go to New York on business for three days in November. The whole family could come with him on the All Aboard family fare on the train. Mamma had sung her way through the evening, talking about all the sights in New York: Greenwich Village and the Statue of Liberty and Rockefeller Center. Everything. She was still singing at Sunday lunch.

After lunch Adam helped dry the dishes. Then he walked out around the back of the house. He was supposed to meet Grayson at the school field at 2:30. That gave him enough time to do some dribbling practice before going. He had practiced for two hours yesterday afternoon and an hour this morning when he first woke up. Of course, he was nowhere near as good as Grayson. Maybe he never would be. But he was sure a whole lot better than he had been two days ago. If only he had begun practicing with Grayson two weeks ago instead of two days ago! But there was no point in thinking about that.

Adam reached the spot where he had left Grayson's soccer ball. It was gone! He had left it at the foot of the blue spruce tree; he was sure. But it wasn't there now. He ran frantically around their small yard. He searched under every bush. He trampled through the remains of his father's summer vegetable garden, kicking aside the brown plants. He couldn't find the ball anywhere.

Adam ran into the house. Catherine was practicing the flute. "Have you seen Grayson's soccer ball?"

Catherine continued playing, tapping her foot in time to the music.

Adam shoved his face in front of hers. "Have you seen my soccer ball?" he shouted.

Catherine stopped playing. "This is 'Jesu, Joy of

Man's Desiring.' It's hard. You shouldn't interrupt me."

"My soccer ball is gone. Do you know where it is?"

"You don't have a soccer ball."

"It's Grayson's."

"Then you shouldn't call it yours."

"It's *gone!* Grayson's soccer ball is gone!"

"Oh, that is a problem." Catherine looked at Adam with sympathy. "That's what happens when you borrow. I borrowed Sissy's skirt for a party last year, and Nora decided it was beautiful, so she cut off the bottom half so it was short enough for her to wear." Catherine sighed. "I guess you'll have to buy Grayson a new ball."

Adam tried to remember if he had ever seen a price tag on a soccer ball in the store. How much did they cost? How long would it take him to earn it? And in the meantime, how could he practice? He needed a ball *today*.

Catherine started playing again.

Adam looked at her in despair. Then he thought of Nora. Of course, Nora! If Nora had cut up Sissy's skirt, Nora could have done any number of things with Grayson's ball. Adam ran up the stairs screaming, "Nora!"

Nora came running out of the bedroom. "Hi, Adam. You need me?"

"Where's Grayson's soccer ball?"

"What's that?"

"A soccer ball. Grayson's soccer ball. I left it in the backyard by the spruce tree. What did you do with it?"

"It's gone?"

"Of course it's gone!" screamed Adam. "I wouldn't be looking for it if it weren't gone."

"I knew it," said Nora. "It was stolen."

"Stolen?" Adam looked at Nora sharply. "Did you take it?"

Nora shook her head. "The vampires did." She nodded her head slowly now. "They heard we were coming to visit them, and they stole the ball."

"What are you talking about?"

"Mamma said so. We're going to see them in New York. And they don't want us to come. So they stole the ball."

Adam grabbed Nora by the shoulders and shook her. "What are you talking about?" he shouted. "Where's the ball?"

Mamma came up the stairs. "Adam, let go of Nora. What's going on?"

"Nora hid Grayson's favorite soccer ball."

Mamma looked confused. "Nora, did you take the soccer ball?"

"No, the vampires did."

"She keeps talking about vampires," said Adam. "She's making it up because she hid the ball and she doesn't want to get in trouble."

Nora shook her head. "I am not making it up. I knew there would be trouble if we went to the Vampire State Building. We shouldn't go there, Mamma. They don't want us to go."

Mamma laughed. "It's the Empire State Building, not the Vampire State Building. It has nothing to do with vampires."

Nora looked doubtful. "Are you sure?"

Mamma put her arms around Nora. "I'm sure. It's just a tall building. There are lots of tall buildings in New York, but this one was the tallest for a long time. You'll like it. Now, Nora, do you know where the soccer ball is?"

"No."

Adam clenched his fists. "You have to know."

Nora looked at Adam hopefully. "Maybe Fancy ate it."

Adam shook his head. His sister was amazingly stupid. She was probably too stupid to have hidden the ball successfully. Adam spent the next hour searching the house, the yard again, the garage. The ball simply wasn't around. He had to leave for the school field without the ball.

"Hi, Grayson." Adam looked at Grayson's lazy body, sprawled in the grass in the sun. Grayson looked happy and relaxed, and now Adam was about to ruin his day. Adam decided to get it over with quick. "I can't find your soccer ball," he blurted out.

"Huh?" Grayson stood up slowly. He stared at Adam with a half-dazed look. "My soccer ball?"

"It disappeared. Maybe my cat ate it."

"Huh?"

"Forget it. I'll find it."

By this time, Grayson was fully awake. "You better find it. It's my best ball."

"I know." Adam kicked the ground so hard a tuft of grass went flying. "I'll find it. Let's practice."

For the next hour they practiced. Grayson was full of even more advice than he'd given on Friday and Saturday. It seemed like every sentence out of his mouth was a rule:

Always kick with the side or top of your foot.

Every kick should be hard.

Pass low.

If you play goalie, don't let them catch you inside the goal. Challenge the other team.

Keep up your speed.

Keep your knees bent when you're passing so no one can kick the ball out from between your legs.

And the most important rule of all: Never think about getting hurt. Just play as hard as you can.

Adam was sweaty and exhausted. His head overflowed with rules. He was better at dribbling than at kicking and passing. "Why do I have to know all this stuff about making goals, anyway? I always play left fullback. That's where Coach Morrison puts me. I'm not even allowed to cross the halfway line. I could never make a goal."

"Coach might make you a forward or a halfback."

"He never would. He's not that stupid," said Adam loudly.

Grayson shook his head. "Even in defense you can cross the halfway line if you're the sweeper and you've got the ball."

"He'll never make me sweeper." Adam looked down at the ball.

"Hey, you're never supposed to look at the ball if you've got it, remember?"

"Too many rules!" Adam stuck his chin out belligerently. "How am I supposed to remember all those rules?"

"You get used to them," said Grayson. "They become natural."

"They won't become natural by tomorrow," shouted Adam.

Grayson turned his back on Adam. Then he suddenly swirled around and kicked the ball out from between Adam's feet. "So what are you going to do, give up?" he shouted back. He dribbled the ball in wider and wider circles around Adam. "You can quit and be the weenie of the class, and I can quit math practice with you and be the dummy of the class. That sound good?"

Adam watched Grayson dribble faster and faster. He didn't want to be the weenie of the class. And Grayson was no dummy. He didn't want anyone ever to think Grayson was the math dummy of the class. "It sounds like puke!" Adam raced at Grayson and went for the ball. He got it. Then they passed the ball between them, up and down the field. Adam shouted out multiplication problems, and Grayson had to shout back the answer before he was allowed to put his foot on the ball again. They went faster and faster and faster.

"Adam, dear, you're home. Did you have a good time? I found this on the porch." Mamma handed Adam a big box covered with wrapping paper.

Adam sat down on the floor and ripped off the paper. He opened the box. Inside was Grayson's soccer ball. But someone had painted yellow flowers all over it. Daisies.

Daisies. It was Kim again. Oh, no.

How was Adam going to explain to Grayson that his best soccer ball, his favorite in the whole world, was now covered with yellow daisies? And how could Kim have done this to Adam?

CHAPTER 11

Holes

· ·

When Adam woke on Monday morning, he knew something was wrong. Terribly, terribly wrong. He had an eerie feeling that was somehow familiar. Everything was quiet, and there was a glistening of wet sun on the window. Suddenly Adam knew what was wrong. He ran to the window. There was a thin layer of snow over everything. He strained his eyes to make out the number on the thermometer. Thirty-five degrees. During the night the temperature had plummeted. And on the one day of the year when he absolutely, positively, definitely had to wear shorts and a short-sleeved shirt. If there was any way Adam was going to have a chance at making the soccer team, he had to have everything working for him. And that meant his freckles had

130

to be out there, with their eyes open, or whatever they had that allowed them to see, and they had to keep him alert, tell him where the ball was. Oh why, oh why did it have to snow today of all days! Why, oh why did he have to live in Michigan!

Adam went back to his bed and sat there, slumped over in depression. He could hear Catherine humming in the bathroom down the hall. He imagined her happily braiding her hair in front of the mirror. He never understood why Catherine was always so cheerful. And there was Nora, busy cutting circles out of an old pillowcase Mamma had given her. She sat on the floor, happy as could be. Adam had watched her doing this before. She made the most lopsided circles imaginable. Then she poked a hole in the middle and shoved her Barbie doll's legs through and admired the awful skirt she had made. Adam thought about how Nora had cut up Sissy's skirt last year. Maybe Nora was going to grow up to be a dress designer. She'd probably die in poverty. But it didn't matter to Nora. She was perfectly happy on the floor, cutting away. *Snip snip snip.* And a hole appeared like magic. Happy Nora. Happy Catherine. Everyone was perfectly happy except Adam. *Snip snip.*

The sun glinted off Nora's scissors. Scissors!

Scissors made holes! Of course, scissors! Adam got off the bed slowly, trying to hide his urgency. He sat down on the floor beside Nora. "That's a nice skirt you're making."

Nora smiled at him. "When I finish, I'm going to make Fancy a hat to cover her ears. It snowed last night."

"I know." Adam thought of poor Fancy with a hat tied in a knot under her chin. "Listen, Nora, could I borrow your scissors for the day?"

Nora looked at Adam, surprised. "Why?"

"Just for something. It doesn't matter."

"Tell me."

"No. Listen, I'll give you some of my bottle caps if you'll let me borrow the scissors."

Nora thought about it awhile. "If I lend you the scissors, I can't make Fancy a hat."

"I'll give you anything you want out of my top drawer."

"Okay," said Nora happily. She handed Adam the scissors. "I want the plastic frog."

"How did you know I have a plastic frog in my drawer?"

"It doesn't matter," said Nora.

"Tell me."

"No."

Adam was half mad at Nora. Then he laughed. "Oh, well. Thanks for the scissors." He opened his top drawer and handed Nora the frog. Then he looked for his transparent tape. He couldn't find it. "My tape's missing."

Nora clutched the frog to her chest and looked down at the rug.

"You know where it is, don't you?"

"I needed it."

Adam controlled his anger. If he yelled at her, she might cry, and then it would take longer to get the tape back. He had to have that tape. "Just give it back."

"It's gone."

"You used it all up?"

Nora nodded. "I'm sorry. I'll ask Mamma to buy more."

"I need it *today*," shouted Adam. He shoved his top drawer shut, pulled open the others, and gathered his clothes together. No tape, he thought. He ran to the bathroom and dressed. No tape. He pulled on his shoes. No tape. No tape. He looked at his new sneakers in despair.

All through breakfast Adam was desperate for a solution. He had rummaged through the kitchen junk drawer and found only thick masking tape and string. He had looked in the sewing cabinet and come up with nothing better than elastic thread. There was no place else he could think of to search: There was no transparent tape in the house. He had to find an alternative. He sat now at the kitchen table and poured himself Rice Chex as his eyes scanned the room frantically.

The phone rang. Catherine dove for it. It was for her. She fiddled with the cord as she talked.

Adam slurped his Rice Chex and looked at that telephone cord. A fine, supple wire was inside that cord. He slurped again.

"Hush!" said Catherine. "That's gross." Then she turned back to her phone call, twisting the cord in and out of her fingers.

Adam slurped once more, but this time with a huge grin on his face.

"Pig!" hissed Catherine.

"I love you," said Adam.

Catherine looked up from her call with amazement on her face.

"You gave me a great idea," said Adam. "Thanks, gorgeous." He kissed her on the cheek as he ran from the kitchen.

He heard Catherine drop the phone behind him.

The garage was dark after the bright light of the

sun reflecting off the snow in the driveway. Adam stood for a moment, letting his eyes adjust. When he could see, he went to the carpenter's bench at the rear. On the pegboard over the bench hung all types of ropes and wires, looped onto hooks. Adam picked a roll of thin black wire, pulled out a length about three feet long, and cut it off with Nora's scissors. He stuffed it in the pocket of his navy blue sweat pants. The black of the wire would hardly show against the navy blue.

Adam walked to school quickly. There were a good ten minutes left before the school bell would ring. He went straight to the boys' bathroom and shut himself in a stall. Nora's scissors felt clumsy in his hand. He cut a big hole in his sweat pants on the front of each knee. Then smaller ones at the back. He had located about twenty really big freckles before he got dressed that morning. Now he carefully cut circles out of his pants so that each of those freckles could see out. It was awkward cutting the circles for the freckles on the back of his legs, but he didn't want to risk taking his pants off. He thought about what problems he had caused himself when he had taken his shirt off in the bathroom the week before.

Once his legs were done, Adam started on his

sweat shirt. It was harder cutting the circles for the freckles on the backs of his arms than it had been for the backs of his legs. He had to make the circles big, to be sure the freckles could see out even if he didn't center the circles properly around each one.

The school bell rang. Adam quickly tied the black wire around his left knee, reaching in through the hole he had cut. Then he pulled the wire up inside his pants and up through his shirt. He wound the other end around the outside of his left ear. When he went out to soccer tryouts that afternoon, he would have to press the very tip of the wire into the inside of his ear. But for now, he left it dangling. He ran to class.

Everyone was seated by the time Adam walked into the classroom. Ms. Werner sat silent, watching him walk down the aisle and hang up his jacket. He could feel her eyes on his back. When he turned around, she was still looking at him. Her mouth hung open and her face had a blank expression. Adam smiled and went to his seat.

He glanced at Kim. She was staring at him, too. Then, slowly, she gave a sort of half smile. Adam could have sworn it was genuinely friendly. He almost smiled back.

Ms. Werner seemed to shake herself to attention.

She cleared her throat. "Let's get started, shall we, class? Who can count for me from zero to a hundred by twos? It's an easy enough job. Who can do it quickly?"

Susanna blurted out, "I can, I can."

Ms. Werner nodded at Susanna. Susanna counted by twos to a hundred. "Good. Now who can count from zero to a hundred by fives?"

William raised his hand. Ms. Werner nodded at William. William counted by fives to a hundred.

"All right, then. Did anyone have any trouble with that?" No one said a thing. Ms. Werner went to the board and drew a red circle with fish in it. Then she pulled a blue piece of chalk out of her box and drew a blue circle with fish in it. "It's Monday morning, and it's our third week of school. So it's time for us to get into something a little bit more challenging. Let's say that each fish in the red school is pregnant, with five little eggs inside her. And let's say that each fish in the blue school is pregnant, with only two little eggs inside her."

Adam looked at the fish. The red ones didn't seem any fatter than the blue ones. But then, fish eggs had to be pretty tiny.

"Keep in mind that you all know how to count by twos and fives, right?" She nodded her head encouragingly. "Now here's our hungry Goldie."

Ms. Werner drew a big yellow fish between the circles of red and blue fish. "Today Goldie is hungry for fish eggs. She wants to eat as many eggs as she can, in gulps of ten eggs at a time. And she must finish a whole circle with no leftovers, as usual. Which circle will Goldie eat?"

Adam liked this problem. It was more fun than the old stuff. Adam figured out that Goldie could finish off the red school of fish in two gulps. There was no point in figuring out how many eggs there were in the blue circle then because Ms. Werner always made the problems so that Goldie could eat only one circle without having leftovers.

Adam leaned back in his seat. He could hear Grayson behind him, scribbling madly on his sheet of paper.

Ms. Werner cleared her throat again. "This isn't really a hard problem; it's just new to you." She smiled brightly. "I didn't expect any of you to get it right away. But I'm sure that all of you can understand it if you approach it systematically. Let's try to work through it together. Milt, how would you go about solving this problem?"

Milt looked up. "I think she'll eat the red circle."

"That's right, Milt." Ms. Werner stood tall, radiating satisfaction. "Why?"

"Because there are more eggs there."

Disappointment flashed across Ms. Werner's face. She gave a little sigh. "But that's not the only thing that matters, right? Why will she eat the red circle?" Ms. Werner looked around the class slowly. "Does anyone know?"

" 'Cause it's got twenty eggs in it, so she can eat in gulps of ten eggs at a time by eating two fish at a time," said Susanna.

"Very good, Susanna. Does anyone else see that?" A few people nodded their heads. Ms. Werner nodded back. "It's just a matter of counting by fives, see? Every two fish over here"—she pointed to the red circle—"make ten eggs, see?" She looked around the room. "All right, class, if you don't understand the problem I just put up, don't worry. You will, soon enough. This year our job is to get you doing multiplication and division fast and easily so you can solve problems like the Goldie problems. I'm going to give you a little quiz now on multiplication. I know most of you haven't practiced your times tables since last spring. But we'll just have this little quiz to see where you are and find out what skills we have to brush up on." Ms. Werner walked up and down the aisles, putting a quiz facedown on each child's desk.

Adam turned around and looked at Grayson.

Grayson grinned at Adam and made the thumbs-up sign.

Adam put the tip of the black wire into his ear just for a second. He heard a low hum. Then silence. Then that hum. Gilbert was snoring. Adam let the wire dangle again. Everything was going fine. Grayson was going to fly through this multiplication test with no problems. And Adam's wire was working, so he had a shot at soccer tryouts. Everything seemed absolutely perfect.

Too perfect, in fact, to last.

CHAPTER 12

Friendship Lost

· ·

"You coming?" Grayson waited for Adam at the edge of the field.

Adam hesitated. He thought of Grayson's ball with daisies all over it. He was going to have to tell Grayson sooner or later, but later seemed better. "I like to go across the bars at recess."

"This is your last chance to practice before tryouts." Grayson rolled a soccer ball under his right foot and waited.

Adam looked past Grayson at the group of boys who had already started playing soccer. At that very moment Clifford looked his way. Adam felt sick in the pit of his stomach. "I don't feel so good. I couldn't keep up with you guys now."

Grayson followed Adam's eyes to the soccer

game. "We can work, just you and me." He scratched his elbow. "You surprised me this weekend. You got a lot better fast."

A lot better, said Adam to himself. "But is a lot better good enough to make the team?"

"You've got a chance. And I sure want you to make it."

"You do? Really?"

"Of course I do." Grayson dribbled a few feet away. "How about practicing passing?"

Adam ran along beside Grayson and received the first pass.

"You nervous about the tryouts?" said Grayson.

Adam stumbled over the ball as he thought about that question. "Yeah, I guess I am."

"I thought so. That why you cut holes in your clothes?"

"Sort of." Adam passed the ball back. He wondered what his freckles were doing at that moment. They had a perfect view through the holes. He hoped they would stay alert at tryouts.

"If you want, you can have my old sweat pants," said Grayson. "My mom bought me new ones. Not that the holes in yours aren't nice or anything."

"Thanks. I might just take them. My mom will probably kill me when she sees what I did to mine."

Adam missed the pass and had to go running after the ball. He took a deep breath; then he finally said it: "Your lost soccer ball showed up again."

"Great!" Grayson jumped in excitement.

Adam tried to act casual. "But it's kind of messed up."

Grayson stopped abruptly. "What happened?"

"It's got daisies painted all over it now."

Grayson's face went red. "Daisies?"

"Yeah."

Grayson's voice rose. "Daisies on my favorite ball?"

Adam shrugged. "I tried to scrub them out with Ajax. They faded a little. Not much, though."

Grayson turned his back on Adam. He picked up the soccer ball and tossed it from hand to hand.

"I'm sorry," said Adam.

Grayson kept his back to Adam.

"I'll get you a new ball," said Adam.

"I don't want a new ball," said Grayson fiercely. He turned around and looked at Adam. He shook his head. "All those weird things you do—tape all over you and holes in your pants and things like that." He pressed on the soccer ball with both hands. "Some of the other guys have been saying you're crazy." Grayson looked away and gulped. "I thought it didn't matter how weird you were. I thought you were nice." He turned back to Adam and his eyes glittered. "I should have known. Guess I really am dumb." He slammed the soccer ball down and it bounced away. "You didn't have the right to paint up my favorite ball. That's it."

"Wait a minute," said Adam, reeling under the force of Grayson's words. "I didn't—"

"Just stay away from me." Grayson ran off.

Adam watched Grayson go, and his stomach felt like ice. He blinked back tears. Then he turned around. Kim stood right behind him. Her face was white. She looked at Adam with big, wet eyes. The tears that Adam felt inside him were running down her cheeks. Adam walked past Kim without a word. He went over to the climbing ladder outside his classroom window. He hung from the first rung.

Suddenly soccer tryouts didn't matter. What mattered was Grayson's friendship. Adam had to find a way to get Grayson to be his friend again. But Grayson was so mad, he'd probably never speak to Adam again. Adam should have told Grayson he thought Kim had painted the ball. He should have shouted it out fast before Grayson ran away. There wouldn't have been anything wrong with telling on Kim. Kim wasn't even Adam's friend. Grayson was

his friend—or had been. Kim wasn't a friend at all.

She wasn't. Sure, she had given him an envelope with violets in it. And a half piece of gum. But that didn't mean they were friends. A friend wouldn't paint daisies on another friend's ball. That was such a stupid thing for her to do. Adam wondered if Kim knew it was Grayson's ball. Maybe she was trying to get him in trouble with Grayson. Or maybe she just thought it was funny to put flowers on the ball. Maybe she even thought it was pretty. When Nora saw the ball, all she could say was how pretty it looked now. When Catherine saw it, she had said, "Not bad." So maybe Kim thought the ball looked better that way. And maybe she was shocked when she found out it was Grayson's ball. Maybe she was crying just now because she had made Grayson hate Adam.

Adam swung hand over hand across the ladder. When he got to the end, he turned and started back. He stopped in the middle of the ladder and looked around. No one was near. No one was looking at him. Grayson was out on the field dribbling the ball, and Clifford was right behind him. Maybe they had planned a nice move. Maybe they'd make a goal together. Oh, if only Adam could have the chance to plan out moves with a team.

Adam made his eyes wander away from the game and on to the bleachers. Kim stood in line behind Julie on the next to the top level of the bleachers. They were waiting for a turn on the round swing that hung from the oak tree. In the grassy area beyond the oak tree, there was lots of activity: several jump ropers, several four-square games, lots of climbers on the monkey bars.

Adam got into action again. He went hand over hand to the end of the ladder. Then back. Hand over hand again. He kept going till he felt exhausted. Even people with great upper-body strength, like Adam, could run out of it. Adam felt weak and limp. Like a tired monkey who had traveled from tree to tree halfway across the Amazon rain forest. He held on tight and closed his eyes. All his problems seemed distant and foreign. He was a monkey. Free and relaxed, hanging in one place in the sun. He was a monkey with no problems worse than fleas. He didn't have to worry about having friends and losing friends.

The metal of the ladder was cold, but not freezing like the ground. Metal absorbed the sun's warmth faster than the ground did because metal was a good conductor. Thinking about conductors made Adam wonder again what his freckles were doing right then. He hung by his right hand and, with his left, he gently poked the end of the black wire a little way into his earhole. He didn't hear a thing. Maybe his freckles were simply enjoying the sun, too.

From where Adam hung now, he couldn't see the bleachers and the round swing anymore. They were behind him. But the freckles on his hands could see everywhere. Adam jumped at Gilbert's voice.

"Susanna's next," said Gilbert. "I bet you ten to one that it's going to happen to her."

There was silence for a moment.

"Well, I guess you're right, Frankie," said Gilbert. "Humphrey says there's still a dozen strands left. They're snapping slowly, one by one. And Susanna's off now. I guess it'll be Melanie, if she takes a long turn. Her or Julie. She's next. Then Kim."

"What?" said Adam. "What are you talking about?"

"Oh, Adam, are you there? I thought you were half asleep." Gilbert snorted in disgust. "You're missing the whole thing. Humphrey, your pinkie freckle, is reporting in."

"Reporting in about what?" said Adam.

"The rope the kids threw over the branch last year to make the swing higher. You know. It rubs against the branch every time anyone swings on it.

And where it rubs, the strands are snapping. One by one. Way up there. The kids on the bleachers can't see it because they're on the wrong side of the branch. But Humphrey sees it all. Wait! He said another one just snapped. He says there's only about five or six minutes left. And no one's doing a thing about it."

"Come on, you going across or not?" said an impatient voice. It was William. He stood at one end of the ladder and waited for his turn to go across the bars. "Hurry up."

Adam dropped from the ladder and rubbed his hands together. He moved aside so that William could go past on the ladder. He was about to head for the bleachers when he saw Grayson.

Grayson stood with his right foot on the soccer ball and his eyes on Adam. He was waiting. Adam felt his chest tighten. Grayson dribbled over to Adam slowly. "Do you know that you talk to yourself?"

"Not to . . ." Adam stopped. He was about to say, "Not to myself, to Gilbert." But then he remembered what Catherine had told him. It was best if no one knew about his freckles. Especially not Grayson, now that Grayson didn't like Adam anymore. Adam looked at Grayson silently. He knew he had to get over to the bleachers fast. But he wanted to talk with Grayson. And, well, it would just take a minute to say what he had to say. And Gilbert had said there were five or six more minutes before the rope would break through. With his left hand, Adam casually brushed at his hair and managed to dislodge the black wire from his ear. He hoped Grayson hadn't noticed.

"You've got to try not to do it at school, okay?" said Grayson, before Adam had a chance to speak. "The other kids talk. Milt saw you, and he told Rick. And William got up behind you because he saw you, too. He wanted to hear what you were saying." Grayson looked down at the ball between his feet. Then he looked at Adam again. "They all think you're weird. Not just a nerd, but weird—like with what you do to your clothes. They'll tease you. And they'll tease me, too, 'cause"—he hesitated—"'cause they think I'm your friend."

"Oh," said Adam.

"Just don't do it at school."

"Right," said Adam.

"And don't do it during soccer tryouts today."

"Right," said Adam.

Grayson looked hard at Adam, as though he wanted to say something more. But he didn't. His eyes were troubled. He sucked his top lip inside his bottom teeth and turned around and walked off.

Adam sighed and watched Grayson, who was already back on the field and dribbling again. Clearly Adam would have to be specially careful for the rest of the day. He'd better tell Gilbert that he wouldn't be tuning in again until the soccer tryout. He took the tip of the black wire and stuck it in his ear again.

"That's it, Frankie," said Gilbert. "The rope is totally frayed. There's only one strand left. Kim's going to drop like a ton of bricks in about five seconds."

One strand left. Kim's going to drop. An eight-foot drop onto that frozen ground! Adam swirled around and ran straight for the round swing, screaming, "Stop!" Kim's rainbow panties were the last thing he saw in the instant before she came crashing down on top of him.

CHAPTER 13

Gilbert

· ·

"You're lucky you fell on your left hand. That makes twice within a week that you've been lucky." Dr. Rizzoli smiled at Adam. "In a couple of days, it won't hurt at all. Just try to go easy on it for a while."

Adam looked at the funny finger splint. Gauze and bandage tape were wrapped around the middle of his hand to hold it in place. It still ached horribly.

"You did a pretty heroic thing, I hear, running over and trying to catch that little girl." Dr. Rizzoli patted Adam on the back. "Because she landed on you, she didn't even get a scratch. Yessiree, that was more than just responsible—that was a gallant act."

Adam didn't feel gallant. He looked at his watch.

It was only 2:10. If he could get his mother to take him back to school, he could still go to tryouts. "There are soccer tryouts today."

"Hmmmm." Dr. Rizzoli studied Adam's face. "Soccer can get pretty rough, and that hand can't take rough stuff."

"You don't use hands in soccer," said Adam. "It's a foul if you do. I've never fouled."

Dr. Rizzoli laughed. "All right. Go for it. But if the hand starts hurting too much or if you knock it at all, stop. Promise?"

"You bet." Adam smiled. "Thanks."

"Any more trouble with the eardrums?"

Trouble? Adam wouldn't call what was going on with his eardrums trouble. "No."

"Good. Well, we better just clean off that leg, okay?"

"What?" Adam looked down. Through the hole in his sweat pants he could see that his left leg was bloody. He looked away. Adam didn't like the sight of blood. "I didn't even notice it."

"That's because your finger pain was so bad. You couldn't think of anything else. Let's just clean it up a bit." Dr. Rizzoli put liquid on a gauze pad. The smell of the medicine made the inside of Adam's nose prickle. Dr. Rizzoli smiled. "Lucky you have these holes in your pants, or I'd have to ask you to take them off." He laughed at his own joke. "This some new fad? My son just bought a pair of jeans for forty dollars that have holes in them and are faded. I thought only teenagers were crazy enough to do things like that." He dabbed around on Adam's shin and then on his knee.

Adam smiled back. The liquid smelled funny, but it didn't burn. His shin didn't hurt at all, and his knee was tender but not bad. Nothing compared to the throbbing in his finger.

"Lost a little skin, that's all." Dr. Rizzoli threw away the gauze pad and put the liquid on a new one. He pressed it onto Adam's knee. "Just a little skin lost. Right here, near this . . . this . . . wire?"

Adam thought of Gilbert right away. "Near the wire?" He hoped this smelly medicine wouldn't interfere with Gilbert's ability to talk.

Dr. Rizzoli looked at Adam inquiringly, but he didn't ask about the wire. "Here, hold this in place," he said, putting Adam's hand over the gauze pad. He opened a drawer under the examination table. "We'll just put a bandage on that wound to keep it clean."

"No," said Adam, thinking of Gilbert's vision. "No, I won't need any bandage."

Dr. Rizzoli held up a square gauze pad. "It won't be too uncomfortable. And if you're worried about this wire you've got here, well, we can just move it above or below the knee."

"I don't need a bandage," said Adam.

"The bandage is necessary, Adam. It'll keep your knee safe from dirt at the soccer tryout."

Adam looked at Dr. Rizzoli. The doctor was determined. All right, Adam would let him put it on. Then he'd take it off for soccer practice. Adam took his hand away from his knee and looked down. He meant to give Gilbert a reassuring look, so the freckle wouldn't worry as the bandage went over him. But when Adam looked at his knee, he had a shock. Right where Gilbert should have been was the wound. Gilbert had come off with the skin.

CHAPTER 14

Soccer Tryouts

"All right, that settles the offense on the blue team." Coach Morrison looked at the chart in his hands. He ran his tongue around the inside of his teeth. "Now for defense. William, you be stopper. Adam, I see you've got something wrong with your hand there."

"I sprained my finger, Coach. It's just a sprain. I can play. The doctor said I can play." Adam stood still with every muscle tense. This had been one awful day so far. First Grayson had decided not to be friends with him anymore, and then Gilbert had died. That was all the bad news Adam could take. Coach Morrison had to let him try out. He just had to. "Listen, my mother even said I could play." Adam didn't tell the coach that he'd had to fight with his mother all the way back from the doctor's before she agreed. The coach didn't need to know that. Adam twisted his hands together. "Please, Coach Morrison."

Coach Morrison rubbed his chin and nodded. "Okay, then let's put you on left fullback, as usual."

"Sure," said Adam.

"Hey, Coach." It was Grayson. He didn't look at Adam, but straight at Coach Morrison. "I think Adam should be the sweeper today."

"Sweeper?" The coach shook his head. "Not this time. Milt, you be sweeper."

Grayson moved closer to the coach. "I really think Adam could do a good job as sweeper."

Coach Morrison studied his chart. "Not right now, Grayson. And Michael, you be right fullback. Gordon, you're goalie. Okay. That's it, guys. First rotation will be at the quarter mark. Let's get the ball rolling."

Grayson didn't look at Adam. He ran to his spot. He was striker today. That meant center of the forwards. Grayson was almost always striker.

Adam thought over what had just happened. Grayson had spoken to the coach about him. He had tried to talk the coach into giving Adam a better position. Adam didn't understand why.

At least Grayson and Adam were on the same

team for tryouts; that was good. And Adam was glad they were on the blue team. Blue was a good color. Red was the color of blood. Adam had had enough blood for today. He bent over and looked at the bandage on his knee.

Gilbert was dead.

Gilbert had been just a funny brown spot on Adam's knee. Not someone with a smile you could remember or eyes you could picture. He was a spot. But he was Adam's spot. He'd been Adam's favorite freckle long before Adam realized he had a personality. And once Adam got to know him, he really liked Gilbert. Gilbert was smart and funny. And now he was dead. One minute a person was alive, and the next minute the person was dead. It could happen to anyone. To Catherine. Or Nora. Or Mamma or Daddy. It could happen to Adam. Adam looked around the soccer field. It could happen to any one of these boys. Adam wanted to shout to them all. He wanted to tell them—what?—something important. Something like "You're alive," or "Be happy," or "Guard your freckles." Anything to make them understand. He wanted all of them to live long and happy lives. And he missed Gilbert already. Poor, lost Gilbert.

And poor, lost Adam. After his mother let him off at school, Adam had wired his right knee and tried to talk Frankie into playing Gilbert's old role. But Frankie hadn't answered him. Adam didn't know whether Frankie was too grief-stricken at Gilbert's death to talk or whether he just wasn't the same kind of freckle leader that Gilbert had been. Whatever, it didn't matter. Adam's freckles were silent. And Adam would have to play this game on his own. He had thrown the black wire away.

Gilbert was dead.

Adam patted his left knee lovingly on top of the bandage. He could imagine what Gilbert would be saying now if he were alive. He would be saying Adam should get in there and play his position close and hard. And Frankie would be saying that Adam should be aggressive and go all over his side of the field. And they would have gone off on a long argument. Adam smiled sadly to himself. He'd never hear them argue again. He sniffled. Well, that was no way to act! He should pull himself together. Like Gilbert would have wanted, he should get in there. He should charge. All right, he would. He'd play as hard as he could. He'd play his heart out for Gilbert's sake.

And there was no better time to start than now. The ball was moving toward Adam. Right toward him. Adam ran into the group of boys and went for

the ball. But Milt got there first. He dribbled and looked around. Adam cleared himself for a pass. It would have been easy for Milt to pass to him. Michael was too far away. But Milt looked away from Adam and passed to Michael. It was a long shot. Michael got it and sent it on to William. And then the ball was with the blue offense and back up the field, past the center line, past where Adam was allowed to cross.

Milt shouldn't have passed to Michael when it would have been so much safer to pass to Adam. He shouldn't have! He shouldn't have taken the risk of such a long pass.

But then, maybe Milt didn't see it that way. Maybe Milt thought Adam couldn't receive the pass, and even if he did, Milt thought Adam couldn't do anything with it. No one did. No one was going to give Adam a chance.

Adam gritted his teeth and stood his ground. He'd show them. He was a boy who had known and loved a freckle. Nothing could stop him. The red team was on the offense now, and the ball made its way toward Adam again. The ball always made its way toward Adam. The red team thought Adam was the weak link in the defense. They thought he was afraid of getting hurt and afraid of throwing himself into the middle of the group and unable to kick or pass or dribble or do anything. Well, they'd find out they were wrong!

Michael ran in to get the ball. But his legs were too far apart; even Adam could see that. Grayson had warned Adam about exactly that problem. The red team kicked the ball right between Michael's legs. Adam forced himself to go smack into the middle of the group. He recovered the ball from behind Michael. He dribbled over to the right, too close to the red sweeper, back into the group; good, there was an opening. He passed to Milt. Milt took it up toward the center, and the red team stole it again. A red forward came running toward Adam with the ball stuck to his feet, as though he was a magnet and the ball was iron. Adam ran out to block him. The forward tried to run past on the left. Adam kicked at the ball. The forward got it back and dribbled in a circle. He passed wide to another red forward. But the pass was slow. Adam knew he could intercept. He ran with all his might. William came from nowhere and got the ball. Adam ran ahead. Pass to me, he called in his head silently. Pass to me, William. Please, please pass to me.

William looked around. He saw Adam in the clear. He looked over at Michael. He stared straight at Michael, then faked out with a pass to Adam. Adam got it. *He got it.* He looked down at the beautiful white-and-black ball between his feet. A red forward kicked it away from him.

Adam ran after the forward. Why had he looked down at the ball? You *never* look at the ball once you have it. Never never never. Adam had made a mistake. Well, it wouldn't happen again.

The ball was over on the other side now. Adam watched excitedly as his own team, the blue team, went for a goal. But the red goalie was good. The ball was coming back this way. The same forward that Adam had blocked the last time had the ball again. Adam charged. But the forward passed immediately to another forward over by Milt. Milt tried to block and failed. The red forward ran on.

Adam ran after them. Michael came in and got the ball. But just for a moment. The red forward had it again. He kicked for a goal. High and hard. Just the way you're supposed to. He made it.

Gordon kicked at the dirt and looked miserable. He had been too far back inside the goal. Adam knew how he felt. Adam had been miserable when he had broken the rule and looked down at the ball and lost it. But poor Gordon had broken the rule and stayed too far inside the goal and cost the team a point. Being goalie was probably the scariest thing in the world.

There wasn't time for feeling sorry, though. The

ball was back in action. Up the field, with the blues running like crazy.

Coach Morrison blew his whistle. "Quarter's up. Come here, guys."

Grayson bumped up against Adam.

Adam looked at Grayson hopefully.

"You're doing okay." Grayson gave a small smile. "I knew you could."

Adam could hardly believe his ears. He grinned so wide his face hurt.

"Hurry up," called Coach Morrison. He shouted over to the boys on the sidelines. "You, too. I need everyone." All the boys crowded around the coach. "It's a good fast scrimmage, guys. I'm proud of you all. Keep it up. Now, blue team, just to make it interesting, let's play with the defense a bit. Stopper and goalie, change places. Left fullback becomes sweeper; sweeper becomes right fullback; right full-back becomes left fullback. You got that? Okay, blue team, go." Coach Morrison scribbled on his chart. "Now, red team . . ."

Adam couldn't hear what Coach Morrison was saying any longer. He was stunned. William was goalie. Gordon was stopper. Michael was left full-back. Milt was right fullback. And Adam, Adam was sweeper!

Adam could have jumped for joy. He did. And,

coming down, jostled his hand. His sprained finger hurt. He had to be careful and not do anything to hurt his finger worse. He didn't want to get cut out of the tryouts because of his hand. He was sweeper. That meant he could get the ball and go with it. He could pass and receive up and down the entire field. He could go with the offense. If only he got the ball, he could go with it.

And he could run beside Grayson. Grayson, who had smiled at him. His friend, Grayson.

The game started and within minutes there was a lot of action on the other side of the field. So much action. And nothing on Adam's side. Adam wanted the ball to come his way. But that was the wrong attitude. He should be glad that his team's offense was doing so well. The blue team was one point behind. It was time to make a goal and catch up. And then go on for more goals and win.

And here came the ball. Faster and faster. And Adam was on top of it. And dribbling. He needed someone to pass to fast. Clifford was behind Adam, backing him up. Clifford, who thought Adam played lousy, was actually backing him up. Adam got so flustered, he tripped. But he didn't lose the ball. Milt was off to the right, but too far for a pass. Adam wasn't sure he could kick fast and hard enough to get a pass through to Milt at that distance.

Then, out of nowhere, there was Grayson beside him. Adam passed. Grayson got it and ran to the right. Adam went straight through the red forwards and was ready when Grayson passed back to him. Gordon came up on the left. There was a red forward challenging Adam. Adam looked at Grayson and faked it. He passed to Gordon. The red forward didn't fall for the fake. He intercepted. He was dribbling fast. Michael came up and got the ball. Passed it to Adam. Adam dribbled as fast as he could. Passed it to Gordon. Good pass this time. And Gordon passed to Grayson.

They were over the center line now. Adam had never crossed the center line in a game before. He felt exhilarated. He ran behind Grayson, then out to the right. Grayson passed. A red forward took it. Adam challenged and got it back. He had a clear shot at a goal now. But he was far. There was Grayson, much closer to the goalposts. Grayson could make this goal. Adam should pass to Grayson. But Adam wanted to make a goal himself. If he made a goal, maybe he'd make the team. But if he missed . . .

Adam passed to Grayson. Grayson kicked. Perfect. A goal!

And Adam was jumping for joy again, despite the pain in his hand, jumping and jumping.

CHAPTER 15

Friends

. . . .

Adam stood on the corner of the school yard, face-to-face with Grayson. "Thanks for all you did," he said.

"You're the one who did it," said Grayson. "You played great."

"Because you're a great teacher," said Adam.

Grayson smiled. "No better than you."

"Let's hope that's true."

"It is," said Grayson. "Ms. Werner passed back the multiplication test while you were at the doctor's."

Adam's eyes went wide. "How'd you do?"

"Ninety-five."

"Way to go!"

"Guess this turned out okay," said Grayson.

"Soccer and math," said Adam, "you and me. Good combinations."

"There are going to be a lot of practices after school," said Grayson. "Being on the team is hard work."

"Yeah," said Adam. "I can't wait."

Grayson laughed. "I guess we'll have to put off our own soccer practice together till the weekend."

"Sounds good," said Adam. He stretched out his right hand, his healthy hand, to Grayson. Grayson took it and shook hard. "See you tomorrow."

"Okay," said Grayson. He turned and loped off.

The four blocks home seemed to fly by. Adam imagined his mother's face as he told her. She would be surprised. Everyone would be surprised.

"Surprise!" Kim jumped out from behind a maple tree, holding a small paper bag in her hand

Adam yelped. Then he gave an embarrassed laugh. "Hi."

"Oh, I forgot." Kim ran back behind the tree. Then she jumped out again, reached into the paper bag, and threw tiny cut-up pieces of colored paper all over Adam. "Surprise!" she shouted.

Adam stared at her. He brushed the little pieces of paper out of his eyebrows and off his nose. "Hi," he whispered.

"I saw your assist." Kim crumpled the empty paper bag and clutched it in both hands. "You were terrific." Her face glowed with pleasure.

Adam smiled in spite of himself. "I made the team."

"I know. I stayed till the end and watched Coach Morrison tell everyone." Kim took a deep breath and twisted the paper bag in her hands. "You deserved it."

"Thanks." Adam began walking.

Kim stuffed the bag into her pocket and fell into step beside him. "I didn't get a chance to talk to you before. You went off to the doctor's so fast, and when you got back, you went straight to the soccer field. So there was no time to talk." She did a little skip. "Thank you for saving me today."

"I didn't do anything. You fell, all the same."

"Oh, you saved me. I know that." Kim marched noisily through the dry leaves on the sidewalk. "And then you went and broke your finger. Just to save me."

"It's only sprained," said Adam. "And I didn't mean to do it."

"But you did," said Kim. She turned around and walked backward beside Adam. "You did. And you did it for me."

"It was an accident," said Adam.

"You knew the rope was going to break before it happened," said Kim. "How did you know?"

"I saw the strands of the rope snapping."

Kim shook her head. "No. I was watching you. I was watching you hanging on the climbing ladder, just swinging in one spot. Your back was to me. Then you jumped off and talked to Grayson. And your back was to me the whole time."

"Maybe I noticed it earlier. Yeah. It was definitely frayed."

"But you ran over just at the right moment," said Kim. "How did you know?"

Adam didn't say anything.

"I'd like to know," said Kim. "I won't tell anyone."

Adam chewed at his bottom lip. He wanted to tell Kim. He wanted to see if she'd believe him. "I saw it when my back was toward you. I saw it . . . with my hands."

"Oh," said Kim. Her voice was full of awe.

"With my pinkie finger, to be precise," said Adam.

"Oh," breathed Kim.

"With a freckle on my pinkie finger, to be exact," said Adam.

"Oh, oh, oh," said Kim.

"Do you believe me?" asked Adam.

"Why shouldn't I?" said Kim. "You saw the spider go up the back of Ms. Werner's leg, and there's no way you could have put it on her. I was watching you. You just knew it was there."

"Are you going to blab on me?" asked Adam.

"Never," said Kim. "Can you do other magic things?"

Adam thought about that. Magic things. He hadn't realized his freckles were magic before. But that's what they were, of course. "No, that's all. I'm just ordinary in every other way."

"Not to me, you're not. To me you're special." Kim tugged at her braids. "Susanna said that you'd gone crazy, and now she would be the best student in the class."

"I didn't go crazy," said Adam.

"No," said Kim. She walked along in silence for a moment. "A freckle on your pinkie can see," she said softly.

"All my freckles can," said Adam. "But my favorite freckle died."

"Oh, no," said Kim.

"He was very funny," said Adam. "He talked real fancy."

"Mmmm," said Kim.

"He helped me at soccer," said Adam. "He would have been so happy to know I made the team. He should have been here."

"To share in the glory," said Kim.

"That's right," said Adam. "I miss him." He sighed. "I liked him a lot."

"How sad. I had a bowl with four goldfish once." Kim nodded. "Fish die, too. It's not the same as freckles, of course. I'm sorry about your freckle." She brushed her braids back over her shoulder and looked at Adam solemnly. "What are you going to do with the soccer ball, the one with daisies all over it?"

"Did you paint the daisies?" asked Adam.

"Do you like them?" asked Kim.

"Well, my sister thinks they're fabulous," said Adam. He didn't add that his sister was five.

"Then I painted them," said Kim.

"Why?"

"Well, it was such an ugly, dirty ball before. Now it's pretty and bright." Kim ran a circle around Adam, then walked beside him quietly again. "I didn't know it was Grayson's ball. I thought it was yours."

Adam didn't say anything.

"Grayson's sort of grouchy," said Kim.

"No, he's not!"

"He sure acted grouchy today when he found out about the daisies on his ball."

"That's his favorite ball," said Adam. "Grayson's not grouchy. He's nice. He's very nice."

"Well, if he's so nice, he'll like the flowers once he sees them," said Kim. "And if he doesn't, I'll help you earn the money to buy him a new ball."

Adam could see his house up ahead. He wondered if anyone in his family was watching. If they saw him with Kim, they might tease him. Would he mind being teased?

"Do you play chess?" asked Kim.

"I watched it once," said Adam.

"Me, too," said Kim. "Want to play it with me sometime?"

"I don't know the rules," said Adam.

"So what?" Kim smiled. "Want to?"

"All right."

"I've got to go now." Kim stopped still.

Adam stopped, too.

"I think your freckles look good," said Kim. "I mean the ones that aren't dead."

"Why are you being so nice to me?"

"What?" said Kim.

"You know, the lizard and the envelope and the package and, well, just everything. I thought you hated me."

"Do you hate me?" asked Kim.

Adam shook his head. Little pieces of colored paper fell down out of his hair like a soft shower. He blew at them. "Why did you do all those things?"

"I don't know." She hesitated. "My mom says sometimes I do things just to get attention. To get noticed, you know?"

"You could have just talked to me," said Adam.

"I tried. Like when you were sitting on the bleachers last week and you had that beetle on you. The one that died in my washing machine. But you didn't want to talk. You kept staring past me." Kim looked down at her feet. Then she looked up and smiled. "Now you notice me."

"Yeah," said Adam. "I sure do notice you."

Kim glanced all around, furtively. Then she whispered, "Look up."

Adam looked up.

Kim gave him a peck kiss on the cheek and ran off.

Adam watched her, not knowing what to think. Kisses were yucky. But Kim wasn't too yucky. Maybe she wasn't yucky at all. She believed in him.

Kim Larkin stood there and listened to Adam talk about his freckles, and she believed him. There might not be anyone else in the whole world who would have believed him. Kim understood Adam in a way no one else did. She accepted him as he was and didn't think he was nuts. Adam felt a sudden warm wave of gratitude toward Kim.

Life was wonderful and amazing.

Adam walked home and went into his house.

Catherine was in the living room practicing flute. She put down the flute and walked up to him. She walked around him silently. She stopped in front of him and looked him up and down. "There are holes all over your clothes and little pieces of paper all over you."

"Yeah," said Adam, grinning. "And I made the team."

CHAPTER 16

Freckles

· ·

Adam stepped into the hot tub. He was filthy, and he ached all over. And he was as happy as he had ever been. The team had just played their first game, and they had tied.

Adam had been on the team for eight days now. Eight glorious days. He still hung back a little when the crowd around the ball got too thick. He had to force himself not to think about getting hurt. But he kept working on that. And he was definitely a good passer now. He and Gordon had formed a habit of backing each other up and trying to feed the ball together to whoever was clear for a shot at a goal—usually Grayson or Clifford or Rick. Yeah, Adam was a good passer. And he was decent at dodging. He still had a long way to go at blocking, though. But that would come in time, too. Adam was definitely getting better at soccer with each day.

After every practice, he came home and did chores. His mother was making him earn the money to buy a new sweat suit because she was still angry about the holes in his clothes. But even that didn't bother Adam.

And on Saturday mornings he and Kim did chores for Kim's mother. They were earning money together. Grayson never did learn to like the daisies but, instead of a new ball, he wanted shin guards and a new water bottle. So Kim and Adam had their work cut out for them.

It was all very exhausting, in a wonderful kind of way. The only sad thing was that Gilbert wasn't around to share in the glory, as Kim had said. Adam had tried talking to Frankie at least a dozen times in the past week. But Frankie wouldn't answer. Adam had rubbed Catherine's body lotion all over both knees, even on his scab, but still Frankie remained silent. It wasn't that Adam wanted his freckles to help him anymore. It was that he missed them, and he was sad about Gilbert, and he wanted to talk to Frankie about missing Gilbert. Surely Frankie must miss Gilbert even more than Adam did. It would help them both if they could talk to each other. But Frankie wouldn't talk.

Adam sat in the tub. The water soothed his tired body. He slid down, careful to hold his left hand out, resting over the edge of the tub. He still had to treat his sprained finger gently or the pain would come throbbing back. Once he was fully relaxed, he sat up. He took the washcloth that hung over the faucet and scrubbed at his feet. Then he moved up his legs. When he got to his knees, he noticed that the scab on his left knee had fallen off during the day.

Adam leaned over so his face was very close to his knee. The new skin that had formed under the scab was pink and shiny. And right smack in the middle of the shiny new skin was a faint brown speck. Adam looked even closer. There was no doubt about it: It was a freckle.

Adam quickly slid into the water till his ears were under. "Gilbert?" he called softly. "Gilbert, is that you?"

No answer.

Adam tapped on his knee with urgency. "Gilbert, Gilbert, wake up."

No answer.

Adam pinched his knee. "Gilbert, is that you? Wake up, please, wake up."

"Persistent, aren't you?" said Gilbert. "And with that obnoxious pinching again."

"Oh, you're back!" Adam laughed out loud. "Whoopee! You're back."

"I never was gone, kid."

"Sure you were. You got scraped off."

Gilbert chuckled. "A little scrape doesn't kill a freckle. I was there all along. It's kind of restful to sleep under a scab for a week or so. Like a well-earned vacation. I enjoyed the break."

"But if you were there, why didn't you answer me?" said Adam.

"Why should I have?" said Gilbert.

"I needed you," said Adam. "I needed you for the tryouts."

"Did you?" asked Gilbert. "Did you really? Think before you answer."

Adam thought. He was on the team. He had made it—with Grayson's help. And with his own hard, hard work. He had made it. Adam had learned how to stay alert all on his own. He didn't need the freckles to tell him when the ball was coming. "Even if I didn't need you," said Adam, "I wanted you. I missed you."

"I suppose I missed you, too." Gilbert lowered his voice to a whisper. "I think even Frankie missed you, though he'd never admit it. He was so excited at the tryouts. Oh, my, yes. It was fun while it lasted."

"What do you mean, 'while it lasted'?" said Adam.

"It's over," said Gilbert.

Adam put his palm over the cap of his knee and held it tight. "For good?"

"Ahhh," said Gilbert. He made a harrumphing noise, as though he were preparing for a speech. He spoke in an elevated tone. "The relationship between a boy and his freckles is extraordinary."

"I know that," said Adam with sincerity.

"Daily encounters don't fit," said Gilbert. "We can't just be your chums. You mustn't treat this special relationship as though it's prosaic."

"What does *prosaic* mean?"

"Ordinary."

"I know you're not ordinary friends," said Adam. "I know that."

"Very well," said Gilbert. "Then you'll understand when I say you are completely self-reliant now; you don't need assistance. And we—regretfully, I admit, given what laughter you've brought to us—we must sign off for now."

"For now?" Adam's chest tightened in hope. "Does that mean you'll talk to me again the next time I need help?"

"Perhaps you won't need assistance in the future."

"But if I do," said Adam, "will you be there for me?"

"Adam, really, my boy. Your ears were sensitized by the lightning. That's why you can hear us now with a conductor. But eventually the effect of the shock will wear off. This sort of thing doesn't last forever."

"How long could it last?"

"I have no idea, actually," said Gilbert.

"Then it might be weeks," said Adam. "Or months. Or years. Maybe when I'm fifteen, I'll still be sliding down into the tub water and hearing you and Frankie arguing."

"That would be eavesdropping!" shouted Frankie.

"Oh, Frankie," said Gilbert. "I didn't know you were awake."

"You're the one who was eavesdropping," said Adam.

"I have a right to listen when it concerns me," said Frankie. "But if you listened in on us in the future, that would be true eavesdropping."

"He has a point," said Gilbert. "You have to promise that you won't try to listen in. It isn't honorable."

"All right," said Adam slowly. "But, Gilbert, if I need you and if my ears are still sensitized, say you'll be there for me when I speak to you."

"We'll see. Don't think about it now."

"Is that the best answer I can get?" said Adam.

Gilbert chuckled. "I've always admired your persistence. Now go to bed, soccer player. You need the sleep. Go on."

"Yeah." Adam closed his eyes and smiled. Gilbert was alive and well. Adam was on the team. Grayson was a friend. Kim was fast becoming a friend. All was right with the world. "Yeah," Adam repeated. He got up, dried off, dressed, and went to the bedroom.

Catherine was in the top bunk, reading. She smiled at him and turned back to her book.

Nora was in her bed, sleeping with her arm around the yellow-daisy soccer ball. Grayson had given it to her when he heard how great she thought it looked. She kept it in Dad's old Army duffel bag in the closet during the day. But at night she slept with it.

Adam climbed into his bed and stuck his head under the edges of the curtain. He looked out at the streetlight and fell into a deep, sweet sleep.